D0458995

ALBUQUERQUE ACADEMY
LIBRARY

$^{11}/_{91}$

ALBUQUERQUE ACADEMY
LIBRARY

Also by
Jamaica Kincaid

At the Bottom of the River
Annie John
A Small Place

LUCY

L U C Y

Jamaica Kincaid

Farrar Straus Giroux

New York

Copyright © 1990 by Jamaica Kincaid
All rights reserved
Printed in the United States of America
Published simultaneously in Canada by
*HarperCollins*CanadaLtd
First edition, 1990
Library of Congress catalog card number 90-83987

FIC
KINCAID

For George W. S. Trow

Contents

LUCY

POOR VISITOR

IT WAS MY FIRST DAY. I had come the night before, a gray-black and cold night before—as it was expected to be in the middle of January, though I didn't know that at the time—and I could not see anything clearly on the way in from the airport, even though there were lights everywhere. As we drove along, someone would single out to me a famous building, an important street, a park, a bridge that when built was thought to be a spectacle. In a day dream I used to have, all these places were points of happiness to me; all these places were lifeboats to my small drowning soul, for I would imagine myself entering and leaving them, and just that—entering and leaving over and over again—would see me through a bad feeling I did not have a name for. I only knew it felt a little like sadness but heavier than

that. Now that I saw these places, they looked ordinary, dirty, worn down by so many people entering
and leaving them in real life, and it occurred to me
that I could not be the only person in the world for
whom they were a fixture of fantasy. It was not my
first bout with the disappointment of reality and it
would not be my last. The undergarments that I
wore were all new, bought for my journey, and as
I sat in the car, twisting this way and that to get a
good view of the sights before me, I was reminded
of how uncomfortable the new can make you feel.

I got into an elevator, something I had never
done before, and then I was in an apartment and
seated at a table, eating food just taken from a refrigerator. In the place I had just come from, I always
lived in a house, and my house did not have a
refrigerator in it. Everything I was experiencing—
the ride in the elevator, being in an apartment, eating day-old food that had been stored in a
refrigerator—was such a good idea that I could
imagine I would grow used to it and like it very
much, but at first it was all so new that I had to
smile with my mouth turned down at the corners.
I slept soundly that night, but it wasn't because I
was happy and comfortable—quite the opposite; it
was because I didn't want to take in anything else.

That morning, the morning of my first day, the morning that followed my first night, was a sunny morning. It was not the sort of bright sun-yellow making everything curl at the edges, almost in fright, that I was used to, but a pale-yellow sun, as if the sun had grown weak from trying too hard to shine; but still it was sunny, and that was nice and made me miss my home less. And so, seeing the sun, I got up and put on a dress, a gay dress made out of madras cloth—the same sort of dress that I would wear if I were at home and setting out for a day in the country. It was all wrong. The sun was shining but the air was cold. It was the middle of January, after all. But I did not know that the sun could shine and the air remain cold; no one had ever told me. What a feeling that was! How can I explain? Something I had always known—the way I knew my skin was the color brown of a nut rubbed repeatedly with a soft cloth, or the way I knew my own name— something I took completely for granted, "the sun is shining, the air is warm," was not so. I was no longer in a tropical zone, and this realization now entered my life like a flow of water dividing formerly dry and solid ground, creating two banks, one of which was my past—so familiar and predictable that even my unhappiness then made me happy now just to think of it—the other my future, a gray blank, an overcast seascape on which rain was falling and no boats were in sight. I was no longer in a tropical zone and I felt cold inside and out, the first time such a sensation had come over me.

In books I had read—from time to time, when the plot called for it—someone would suffer from homesickness. A person would leave a not very nice situation and go somewhere else, somewhere a lot better, and then long to go back where it was not very nice. How impatient I would become with such a person, for I would feel that I was in a not very nice situation myself, and how I wanted to go some-where else. But now I, too, felt that I wanted to be back where I came from. I understood it, I knew where I stood there. If I had had to draw a picture of my future then, it would have been a large gray patch surrounded by black, blacker, blackest. What a surprise this was to me, that I longed to be back in the place that I came from, that I longed to sleep in a bed I had outgrown, that I longed to be with people whose smallest, most natural ges-ture would call up in me such a rage that I longed to see them all dead at my feet. Oh, I had imagined that with my one swift act—leaving home and coming to this new place—I could leave behind me, as if it were an old garment never to be worn again, my sad thoughts, my sad feelings, and my discontent with life in general as it presented itself to me. In the past, the thought of being in my present situation had been a comfort, but now I did not even have this to look forward to, and so I lay down on my bed and dreamt I was eating a bowl of pink mullet and green figs cooked in coconut milk, and it had been cooked by my grandmother, which was why the taste of it pleased me so, for she was the person I liked best in all the world and those were the things I liked best to eat also.

The room in which I lay was a small room just off the kitchen—the maid's room. I was used to a small room, but this was a different sort of small room. The ceiling was very high and the walls went all the way up to the ceiling, enclosing the room like a box—a box in which cargo traveling a long way should be shipped. But I was not cargo. I was only an unhappy young woman living in a maid's room, and I was not even the maid. I was the young girl who watches over the children and goes to school at night. How nice everyone was to me, though, saying that I should regard them as my family and make myself at home. I believed them to be sincere, for I knew that such a thing would not be said to a member of their real family. After all, aren't family the people who become the millstone around your life's neck? On the last day I spent at home, my cousin—a girl I had known all my life, an unpleasant person even before her parents forced her to become a Seventh-Day Adventist—made a farewell present to me of her own Bible, and with it she made a little speech about God and goodness and blessings. Now it sat before me on a dresser, and I remembered how when we were children we would sit under my house and terrify and torment each other by reading out loud passages from the Book of Revelation, and I wondered if ever in my whole life a day would go by when these people I had left behind, my own family, would not appear before me in one way or another.

There was also a small radio on this dresser, and I had turned it on. At that moment, almost as if to sum up how I was feeling, a song came on, some of the words of which were "Put yourself in my place, if only for a day; see if you can stand the awful emptiness inside." I sang these words to myself over and over, as if they were a lullaby, and I fell asleep again. I dreamt then that I was holding in my hands one of my old cotton-flannel nightgowns, and

it was printed with beautiful scenes of children playing with Christmas-tree decorations. The scenes
printed on my nightgown were so real that I could
actually hear the children laughing. I felt compelled
to know where this nightgown came from, and I
started to examine it furiously, looking for the label.
I found it just where a label usually is, in the back,
and it read "Made in Australia." I was awakened
from this dream by the actual maid, a woman who
had let me know right away, on meeting me, that
she did not like me, and gave as her reason the way
I talked. I thought it was because of something else,
but I did not know what. As I opened my eyes, the
word "Australia" stood between our faces, and I remembered then that Australia was settled as a prison
for bad people, people so bad that they couldn't be
put in a prison in their own country.

My waking hours soon took on a routine. I
walked four small girls to their school, and when
they returned at midday I gave them a lunch of soup
from a tin, and sandwiches. In the afternoon, I read
to them and played with them. When they were
away, I studied my books, and at night I went to
school. I was unhappy. I looked at a map. An ocean
stood between me and the place I came from, but

would it have made a difference if it had been a teacup of water? I could not go back.

Outside, always it was cold, and everyone said that it was the coldest winter they had ever experienced; but the way they said it made me think they said this every time winter came around. And I couldn't blame them for not really remembering each year how unpleasant, how unfriendly winter weather could be. The trees with their bare, still limbs looked dead, and as if someone had just placed them there and planned to come back and get them later; all the windows of the houses were shut tight, the way windows are shut up when a house will be empty for a long time; when people walked on the streets they did it quickly, as if they were doing something behind someone's back, as if they didn't want to draw attention to themselves, as if being out in the cold too long would cause them to dissolve. How I longed to see someone lingering on a corner, trying to draw my attention to him, trying to engage me in conversation, someone complaining to himself in a voice I could overhear about a God whose love and mercy fell on the just and the unjust.

I wrote home to say how lovely everything was, and I used flourishing words and phrases, as if I were living life in a greeting card—the kind that has a satin ribbon on it, and quilted hearts and roses, and is expected to be so precious to the person receiving it that the manufacturer has placed a leaf of plastic on the front to protect it. Everyone I wrote to said how nice it was to hear from me, how nice it was to know that I was doing well, that I was very much missed, and that they couldn't wait until the day came when I returned.

One day the maid who said she did not like me because of the way I talked told me that she was sure I could not dance. She said that I spoke like a nun, I walked like one also, and that everything about me was so pious it made her feel at once sick to her stomach and sick with pity just to look at me. And so, perhaps giving way to the latter feeling, she said that we should dance, even though she was quite sure I didn't know how. There was a little portable record-player in my room, the kind that when closed up looked like a ladies' vanity case, and she put on a record she had bought earlier that day. It was a song that was very popular at the time—three girls, not older than I was, singing in harmony and in a very insincere and artificial way about love and so on. It was very beautiful all the same, and it was beautiful because it was so insincere and artificial.

She enjoyed this song, singing at the top of her voice, and she was a wonderful dancer—it amazed me to see the way in which she moved. I could not join her and I told her why: the melodies of her song were so shallow, and the words, to me, were meaningless. From her face, I could see she had only one feeling about me: how sick to her stomach I made her. And so I said that I knew songs, too, and I burst into a calypso about a girl who ran away to Port-of-Spain, Trinidad, and had a good time, with no regrets.

The household in which I lived was made up of a husband, a wife, and the four girl children. The husband and wife looked alike and their four children looked just like them. In photographs of themselves, which they placed all over the house, their six yellow-haired heads of various sizes were bunched as if they were a bouquet of flowers tied together by an unseen string. In the pictures, they smiled out at the world, giving the impression that they found everything in it unbearably wonderful. And it was not a farce, their smiles. From wherever they had gone, and they seemed to have been all over the world, they brought back some tiny memento, and they could each recite its history from its very beginnings. Even when a little rain fell, they would admire the way it streaked through the blank air.

At dinner, when we sat down at the table—and did not have to say grace (such a relief; as if they believed in a God that did not have to be thanked every time you turned around)—they said such nice things to each other, and the children were so happy. They would spill their food, or not eat any of it at all, or make up rhymes about it that would end with the words "smelt bad." How they made me laugh, and I wondered what sort of parents I must have had, for even to think of such words in their presence I would have been scolded severely, and I vowed that if I ever had children I would make sure that the first words out of their mouths were bad ones.

It was at dinner one night not long after I began to live with them that they began to call me the Visitor. They said I seemed not to be a part of things, as if I didn't live in their house with them, as if they weren't like a family to me, as if I were just passing through, just saying one long Hallo!, and soon would be saying a quick Goodbye! So long! It was very nice! For look at the way I stared at them as they ate, Lewis said. Had I never seen anyone put a forkful of French-cut green beans in his mouth before? This made Mariah laugh, but almost everything Lewis said made Mariah happy and so she would laugh. I didn't laugh, though, and Lewis looked at me, concern on his face. He said, "Poor Visitor, poor Visitor," over and over, a sympathetic tone to his voice, and then he told me a story about an uncle he had who had gone to Canada and raised monkeys, and of how after a while the uncle loved monkeys so much and was so used to being around them that he found actual human beings hard to take. He had told me this story about his uncle before, and while he was telling it to me this time I was remembering a dream I had had about them: Lewis was chasing me around the house. I wasn't wearing any clothes. The ground on which I was running was yellow, as if it had been paved with cornmeal. Lewis was chasing me around and around the house, and though he came close he could never catch up with me. Mariah stood at the open windows saying, Catch her, Lewis, catch her. Eventually I fell down a hole, at the bottom of which were some silver and blue snakes.

When Lewis finished telling his story, I told them my dream. When I finished, they both fell silent. Then they looked at me and Mariah cleared her throat, but it was obvious from the way she did it that her throat did not need clearing at all. Their two yellow heads swam toward each other and, in unison, bobbed up and down. Lewis made a clucking noise, then said, Poor, poor Visitor. And Mariah said, Dr. Freud for Visitor, and I wondered why she said that, for I did not know who Dr. Freud was. Then they laughed in a soft, kind way. I had meant by telling them my dream that I had taken them in, because only people who were very important to me had ever shown up in my dreams. I did not know if they understood that.

MARIAH

ONE MORNING IN EARLY MARCH, Mariah said to me, "You have never seen spring, have you?" And she did not have to await an answer, for she already knew. She said the word "spring" as if spring were a close friend, a friend who had dared to go away for a long time and soon would reappear for their passionate reunion. She said, "Have you ever seen daffodils pushing their way up out of the ground? And when they're in bloom and all massed together, a breeze comes along and makes them do a curtsy to the lawn stretching out in front of them. Have you ever seen that? When I see that, I feel so glad to be alive." And I thought, So Mariah is made to feel alive by some flowers bending in the breeze. How does a person get to be that way?

I remembered an old poem I had been made

to memorize when I was ten years old and a pupil
at Queen Victoria Girls' School. I had been made
to memorize it, verse after verse, and then had recited the whole poem to an auditorium full of parents, teachers, and my fellow pupils. After I was
done, everybody stood up and applauded with an
enthusiasm that surprised me, and later they told
me how nicely I had pronounced every word, how
I had placed just the right amount of special em-
phasis in places where that was needed, and how
proud the poet, now long dead, would have been to
hear his words ringing out of my mouth. I was then
at the height of my two-facedness: that is, outside I
seemed one way, inside I was another; outside false,
inside, true. And so I made pleasant little noises that
showed both modesty and appreciation, but inside
I was making a vow to erase from my mind, line by
line, every word of that poem. The night after I had
recited the poem, I dreamt, continuously it seemed,
that I was being chased down a narrow cobbled street
by bunches and bunches of those same daffodils that
I had vowed to forget, and when finally I fell down
from exhaustion they all piled on top of me, until
I was buried deep underneath them and was never
seen again. I had forgotten all of this until Mariah
mentioned daffodils, and now I told it to her with

such an amount of anger I surprised both of us. We were standing quite close to each other, but as soon as I had finished speaking, without a second of deliberation we both stepped back. It was only one step that was made, but to me it felt as if something that I had not been aware of had been checked.

Mariah reached out to me and, rubbing her hand against my cheek, said, "What a history you have." I thought there was a little bit of envy in her voice, and so I said, "You are welcome to it if you like."

After that, each day, Mariah began by saying, "As soon as spring comes," and so many plans would follow that I could not see how one little spring could contain them. She said we would leave the city and go to the house on one of the Great Lakes, the house where she spent her summers when she was a girl. We would visit some great gardens. We would visit the zoo—a nice thing to do in springtime; the children would love that. We would have a picnic in the park as soon as the first unexpected and unusually warm day arrived. An early-evening walk in the spring air—that was something she really wanted to do with me, to show me the magic of a spring sky.

On the very day it turned spring, a big snowstorm came, and more snow fell on that day than

ALBUQUERQUE ACADEMY
LIBRARY

had fallen all winter. Mariah looked at me and shrugged her shoulders. "How typical," she said, giving the impression that she had just experienced a personal betrayal. I laughed at her, but I was really wondering, How do you get to be a person who is made miserable because the weather changed its mind, because the weather doesn't live up to your expectations? How do you get to be that way?

While the weather sorted itself out in various degrees of coldness, I walked around with letters from my family and friends scorching my breasts. I had placed these letters inside my brassiere, and carried them around with me wherever I went. It was not from feelings of love and longing that I did this; quite the contrary. It was from a feeling of hatred. There was nothing so strange about this, for isn't it so that love and hate exist side by side? Each letter was a letter from someone I had loved at one time without reservation. Not too long before, out of politeness, I had written my mother a very nice letter, I thought, telling her about the first ride I had taken in an underground train. She wrote back to me, and after I read her letter, I was afraid to even put my face outside the door. The letter was filled with detail after detail of horrible and vicious things she had read or heard about that had taken place on those very same underground trains on which I traveled. Only the other day, she wrote, she had read of an immigrant girl, someone my age exactly, who had had her throat cut while she was a passenger on perhaps the very same train I was riding.

But, of course, I had already known real fear. I had known a girl, a schoolmate of mine, whose father had dealings with the Devil. Once, out of curiosity, she had gone into a room where her father did his business, and she had looked into things that she should not have, and she became possessed. She took sick, and we, my other schoolmates and I, used to stand in the street outside her house on our way home from school and hear her being beaten by what possessed her, and hear her as she cried out from the beatings. Eventually she had to cross the sea, where the Devil couldn't follow her, because the Devil cannot walk over water. I thought of this as I felt the sharp corners of the letters cutting into the skin over my heart. I thought, On the one hand there was a girl being beaten by a man she could not see; on the other there was a girl getting her throat cut by a man she could see. In this great big world, why should my life be reduced to these two possibilities?

L U C Y

When the snow fell, it came down in thick, heavy glops, and hung on the trees like decorations ordered for a special occasion—a celebration no one had heard of, for everybody complained. In all the months that I had lived in this place, snowstorms had come and gone and I had never paid any attention, except to feel that snow was an annoyance when I had to make my way through the mounds of it that lay on the sidewalk. My parents used to go every Christmas Eve to a film that had Bing Crosby standing waist-deep in snow and singing a song at the top of his voice. My mother once told me that seeing this film was among the first things they did when they were getting to know each other, and at the time she told me this I felt strongly how much I no longer liked even the way she spoke; and so I said, barely concealing my scorn, "What a religious experience that must have been." I walked away quickly, for my thirteen-year-old heart couldn't bear to see her face when I had caused her pain, but I couldn't stop myself.

In any case, this time when the snow fell, even I could see that there was something to it—it had a certain kind of beauty; not a beauty you would wish for every day of your life, but a beauty you could appreciate if you had an excess of beauty to begin with. The days were longer now, the sun set later, the evening sky seemed lower than usual, and the snow was the color and texture of a half-cooked egg white, making the world seem soft and lovely and —unexpectedly, to me—nourishing. That the world I was in could be soft, lovely, and nourishing was more than I could bear, and so I stood there and wept, for I didn't want to love one more thing in my life, didn't want one more thing that could make my heart break into a million little pieces at my feet. But all the same, there it was, and I could not do much about it; for even I could see that I was too young for real bitterness, real regret, real hard-heartedness.

The snow came and went more quickly than usual. Mariah said that the way the snow vanished, as if some hungry being were invisibly swallowing it up, was quite normal for that time of year. Everything that had seemed so brittle in the cold of winter—sidewalks, buildings, trees, the people themselves—seemed to slacken and sag a bit at the seams. I could now look back at the winter. It was my past, so to speak, my first real past—a past that was my own and over which I had the final word. I had just lived through a bleak and cold time, and it is not to the weather outside that I refer. I had lived through this time, and as the weather changed from cold to warm it did not bring me along with it. Something settled inside me, something heavy and hard. It stayed there, and I could not think of one thing to make it go away. I thought, So this must be living, this must be the beginning of the time people later refer to as "years ago, when I was young."

My mother had a friendship with a woman— a friendship she did not advertise, for this woman had spent time in jail. Her name was Sylvie; she had a scar on her right cheek, a human-teeth bite. It was as if her cheek were a half-ripe fruit and someone had bitten into it, meaning to eat it, but then realized it wasn't ripe enough. She had gotten into a big quarrel with another woman over this: which of the two of them a man they both loved should live with. Apparently Sylvie said something that was unforgivable, and the other woman flew into an even deeper rage and grabbed Sylvie in an embrace, only it was not an embrace of love but an embrace of hatred, and she left Sylvie with the marked cheek. Both women were sent to jail for public misconduct, and going to jail was something that for the rest of their lives no one would let them forget. It was because of this that I was not allowed to speak to Sylvie, that she was not allowed to visit us when my father was at home, and that my mother's friendship with her was supposed to be a secret. I used to observe Sylvie, and I noticed that whenever she stopped to speak, even in the briefest conversation, immediately her hand would go up to her face and caress her little rosette (before I knew what it was, I was sure that the mark on her face was a rose she had put there on purpose because she loved the beauty of roses so much she wanted to wear one on her face), and it was as if the mark on her face bound her to something much deeper than its reality, something that she could not put into words. One day, outside my mother's presence, she admired the way my corkscrew plaits fell around my neck, and then she said something that I did not hear, for she began by saying, "Years ago when I was young," and she pinched up her scarred cheek with her fingers and twisted it until I thought it would fall off like a dark, purple plum in the middle of her pink palm, and her voice became heavy and hard, even though she was laughing all the time she spoke. That is how I came to think that heavy and hard was the beginning of living, real living; and though I might not end up with a mark on my cheek, I had no doubt that I would end up with a mark somewhere.

L U C Y

. . .

I was standing in front of the kitchen sink one day, my thoughts centered, naturally, on myself, when Mariah came in—danced in, actually—singing an old song, a song that was popular when her mother was a young woman, a song she herself most certainly would have disliked when she was a young woman and so she now sang it with an exaggerated tremor in her voice to show how ridiculous she still found it. She twirled herself wildly around the room and came to a sharp stop without knocking over anything, even though many things were in her path.

She said, "I have always wanted four children, four girl children. I love my children." She said this clearly and sincerely. She said this without doubt on the one hand or confidence on the other. Mariah was beyond doubt or confidence. I thought, Things must have always gone her way, and not just for her but for everybody she has ever known from eternity; she has never had to doubt, and so she has never had to grow confident; the right thing always happens to her; the thing she wants to happen happens. Again I thought, How does a person get to be that way?

Mariah said to me, "I love you." And again she said it clearly and sincerely, without confidence or doubt. I believed her, for if anyone could love a young woman who had come from halfway around the world to help her take care of her children, it was Mariah. She looked so beautiful standing there in the middle of the kitchen. The yellow light from the sun came in through a window and fell on the pale-yellow linoleum tiles of the floor, and on the walls of the kitchen, which were painted yet another shade of pale yellow, and Mariah, with her pale-yellow skin and yellow hair, stood still in this almost celestial light, and she looked blessed, no blemish or mark of any kind on her cheek or anywhere else, as if she had never quarreled with anyone over a man or over anything, would never have to quarrel at all, had never done anything wrong and had never been to jail, had never had to leave anywhere for any reason other than a feeling that had come over her. She had washed her hair that morning and from where I stood I could smell the residue of the perfume from the shampoo in her hair. Then underneath that I could smell Mariah herself. The smell of Mariah was pleasant. Just that—pleasant. And I thought, But that's the trouble with Mariah—she smells pleasant. By then I already knew that I wanted to have a powerful odor and would not care if it gave offense.

L U C Y

. . .

On a day on which it was clear that there was no turning back as far as the weather was concerned, that the winter season was over and its return would be a noteworthy event, Mariah said that we should prepare to go and spend some time at the house on the shore of one of the Great Lakes. Lewis would not accompany us. Lewis would stay in town and take advantage of our absence, doing things that she and the children would not enjoy doing with him. What these things were I could not imagine. Mariah said we would take a train, for she wanted me to experience spending the night on a train and waking up to breakfast on the train as it moved through freshly plowed fields. She made so many arrangements—I had not known that just leaving your house for a short time could be so complicated.

Early that afternoon, because the children, my charges, would not return home from school until three, Mariah took me to a garden, a place she described as among her favorites in the world. She covered my eyes with a handkerchief, and then, holding me by the hand, she walked me to a spot in a clearing. Then she removed the handkerchief and said, "Now, look at this." I looked. It was a big

area with lots of thick-trunked, tall trees along wind-
ing paths. Along the paths and underneath the trees
were many, many yellow flowers the size and shape
of play teacups, or fairy skirts. They looked like
something to eat and something to wear at the same
time; they looked beautiful; they looked simple, as
if made to erase a complicated and unnecessary idea.
I did not know what these flowers were, and so it
was a mystery to me why I wanted to kill them. Just
like that. I wanted to kill them. I wished that I had
an enormous scythe; I would just walk down the
path, dragging it alongside me, and I would cut these
flowers down at the place where they emerged from
the ground.

Mariah said, "These are daffodils. I'm sorry
about the poem, but I'm hoping you'll find them
lovely all the same."

There was such joy in her voice as she said this,
such a music, how could I explain to her the feeling
I had about daffodils—that it wasn't exactly daffodils, but that they would do as well as anything else?
Where should I start? Over here or over there? Anywhere would be good enough, but my heart and my
thoughts were racing so that every time I tried to
talk I stammered and by accident bit my own tongue.

Mariah, mistaking what was happening to me

for joy at seeing daffodils for the first time, reached out to hug me, but I moved away, and in doing that I seemed to get my voice back. I said, "Mariah, do you realize that at ten years of age I had to learn by heart a long poem about some flowers I would not see in real life until I was nineteen?"

As soon as I said this, I felt sorry that I had cast her beloved daffodils in a scene she had never considered, a scene of conquered and conquests; a scene of brutes masquerading as angels and angels portrayed as brutes. This woman who hardly knew me loved me, and she wanted me to love this thing— a grove brimming over with daffodils in bloom— that she loved also. Her eyes sank back in her head as if they were protecting themselves, as if they were taking a rest after some unexpected hard work. It wasn't her fault. It wasn't my fault. But nothing could change the fact that where she saw beautiful flowers I saw sorrow and bitterness. The same thing could cause us to shed tears, but those tears would not taste the same. We walked home in silence. I was glad to have at last seen what a wretched daffodil looked like.

When the day came for us to depart to the house on the Great Lake, I was sure that I did not want to go, but at midmorning I received a letter from my mother bringing me up to date on things she thought I would have missed since I left home and would certainly like to know about. "It still has not rained since you left," she wrote. "How fascinating," I said to myself with bitterness. It had not rained once for over a year before I left. I did not care about that any longer. The object of my life now was to put as much distance between myself and the events mentioned in her letter as I could manage. For I felt that if I could put enough miles between me and the place from which that letter came, and if I could put enough events between me and the events mentioned in the letter, would I not be free to take everything just as it came and not see hundreds of years in every gesture, every word spoken, every face?

On the train, we settled ourselves and the children into our compartments—two children with Mariah, two children with me. In one of the few films I had seen in my life so far, some people on a train did this—settled into their compartments. And so I suppose I should have felt excitement at doing something I had never done before and had only seen done in a film. But almost everything I did now was something I had never done before, and so the new was no longer thrilling to me unless it reminded me of the past. We went to the dining car to eat our dinner. We sat at tables—the children by themselves. They had demanded that, and had said to Mariah that they would behave, even though it was well known that they always did. The other people sitting down to eat dinner all looked like Mariah's relatives; the people waiting on them all looked like mine. The people who looked like my relatives were all older men and very dignified, as if they were just emerging from a church after Sunday service. On closer observation, they were not at all like my relatives; they only looked like them. My relatives always gave backchat. Mariah did not seem to notice what she had in common with the other diners, or what I had in common with the waiters. She acted in her usual way, which was that the world was round and we all agreed on that, when I knew that the world was flat and if I went to the edge I would fall off.

That night on the train was frightening. Every time I tried to sleep, just as it seemed that I had finally done so, I would wake up sure that thousands of people on horseback were following me, chasing me, each of them carrying a cutlass to cut me up into small pieces. Of course, I could tell it was the sound of the wheels on the tracks that inspired this nightmare, but a real explanation made no difference to me. Early that morning, Mariah left her own compartment to come and tell me that we were passing through some of those freshly plowed fields she loved so much. She drew up my blind, and when I saw mile after mile of turned-up earth, I said, a cruel tone to my voice, "Well, thank God I didn't have to do that." I don't know if she understood what I meant, for in that one statement I meant many different things.

When we got to our destination, a man Mariah had known all her life, a man who had always done things for her family, a man who came from Sweden, was waiting for us. His name was Gus, and the way Mariah spoke his name it was as if he belonged to her deeply, like a memory. And, of course, he was a part of her past, her childhood: he was there, apparently, when she took her first steps; she had caught her first fish in a boat with him; they had been in a storm on the lake and their survival was a miracle, and so on. Still, he was a real person, and I thought Mariah should have long separated the person Gus standing in front of her in the present

from all the things he had meant to her in the past.
I wanted to say to him, "Do you not hate the way
she says your name, as if she owns you?" But then
I thought about it and could see that a person coming
from Sweden was a person altogether different from
a person like me.

We drove through miles and miles of countryside, miles and miles of nothing. I was glad not to
live in a place like this. The land did not say, "Welcome. So glad you could come." It was more, "I
dare you to stay here." At last we came to a small
town. As we drove through it, Mariah became ex-
cited; her voice grew low, as if what she was saying
only she needed to hear. She would exclaim with
happiness or sadness, depending, as things passed
before her. In the half a year or so since she had
last been there, some things had changed, some
things had newly arrived, and some things had vanished completely. As she passed through this town,
she seemed to forget she was the wife of Lewis and
the mother of four girl children. We left the small
town and a silence fell on everybody, and in my
own case I felt a kind of despair. I felt sorry for
Mariah; I knew what she must have gone through,
seeing her past go swiftly by in front of her. What
an awful thing that is, as if the ground on which

you are standing is being slowly pulled out from under your feet and beneath is nothing, a hole through which you fall forever.

The house in which Mariah had grown up was beautiful, I could immediately see that. It was large, sprawled out, as if rooms had been added onto it when needed, but added on all in the same style. It was modeled on the farmhouse that Mariah's grandfather grew up in, somewhere in Scandinavia. It had a nice veranda in front, a perfect place from which to watch rain fall. The whole house was painted a soothing yellow with white trim, which from afar looked warm and inviting. From my room I could see the lake. I had read of this lake in geography books, had read of its origins and its history, and now to see it up close was odd, for it looked so ordinary, gray, dirty, unfriendly, not a body of water to make up a song about. Mariah came in, and seeing me studying the water she flung her arms around me and said, "Isn't it great?" But I wasn't thinking that at all. I slept peacefully, without any troubling dreams to haunt me; it must have been that knowing there was a body of water outside my window, even though it was not the big blue sea I was used to, brought me some comfort.

Mariah wanted all of us, the children and me,

to see things the way she did. She wanted us to enjoy the house, all its nooks and crannies, all its sweet smells, all its charms, just the way she had done as a child. The children were happy to see things her way. They would have had to be four small versions of myself not to fall at her feet in adoration. But I already had a mother who loved me, and I had come to see her love as a burden and had come to view with horror the sense of self-satisfaction it gave my mother to hear other people comment on her great love for me. I had come to feel that my mother's love for me was designed solely to make me into an echo of her; and I didn't know why, but I felt that I would rather be dead than become just an echo of someone. That was not a figure of speech. Those thoughts would have come as a complete surprise to my mother, for in her life she had found that her ways were the best ways to have, and she would have been mystified as to how someone who came from inside her would want to be anyone different from her. I did not have an answer to this myself. But there it was. Thoughts like these had brought me to be sitting on the edge of a Great Lake with a woman who wanted to show me her world and hoped that I would like it, too. Sometimes there is no escape, but often the effort of trying will do quite nicely for a while.

I was sitting on the veranda one day with these thoughts when I saw Mariah come up the path, holding in her hands six grayish-blackish fish. She said, "Taa-daah! Trout!" and made a big sweep with her hands, holding the fish up in the light, so that rainbowlike colors shone on their scales. She sang out, "I will make you fishers of men," and danced around me. After she stopped, she said, "Aren't they beautiful? Gus and I went out in my old boat—my very, very old boat—and we caught them. My fish. This is supper. Let's go feed the minions."

It's possible that what she really said was "millions," not "minions." Certainly she said it in jest. But as we were cooking the fish, I was thinking about it. "Minions." A word like that would haunt someone like me; the place where I came from was a dominion of someplace else. I became so taken with the word "dominion" that I told Mariah this story: When I was about five years old or so, I had read to me for the first time the story of Jesus Christ feeding the multitudes with seven loaves and a few fishes. After my mother had finished reading this to me, I said to her, "But how did Jesus serve the fish?

boiled or fried?" This made my mother look at me in amazement and shake her head. She then told everybody she met what I had said, and they would shake their heads and say, "What a child!" It wasn't really such an unusual question. In the place where I grew up, many people earned their living by being fishermen. Often, after a fisherman came in from sea and had distributed most of his fish to people with whom he had such an arrangement, he might save some of them, clean and season them, and build a fire, and he and his wife would fry them at the seashore and put them up for sale. It was quite a nice thing to sit on the sand under a tree, seeking refuge from the hot sun, and eat a perfectly fried fish as you took in the view of the beautiful blue sea, former home of the thing you were eating. When I had inquired about the way the fish were served with the loaves, to myself I had thought, Not only would the multitudes be pleased to have some-thing to eat, not only would they marvel at the miracle of turning so little into so much, but they might go on to pass a judgment on the way the food tasted. I know it would have mattered to me. In our house, we all preferred boiled fish. It was a pity that the people who recorded their life with Christ never mentioned this small detail, a detail that would have meant a lot to me.

When I finished telling Mariah this, she looked at me, and her blue eyes (which I would have found beautiful even if I hadn't read millions of books in which blue eyes were always accompanied by the word "beautiful") grew dim as she slowly closed the lids over them, then bright again as she opened them wide and then wider.

A silence fell between us; it was a deep silence, but not too thick and not too black. Through it we could hear the clink of the cooking utensils as we cooked the fish Mariah's way, under flames in the oven, a way I did not like. And we could hear the children in the distance screaming—in pain or pleasure, I could not tell.

Mariah and I were saying good night to each other the way we always did, with a hug and a kiss, but this time we did it as if we both wished we hadn't gotten such a custom started. She was almost out of the room when she turned and said, "I was looking forward to telling you that I have Indian blood, that the reason I'm so good at catching fish and hunting birds and roasting corn and doing all sorts of things

is that I have Indian blood. But now, I don't know
why, I feel I shouldn't tell you that. I feel you will
take it the wrong way."

This really surprised me. What way should I
take this? Wrong way? Right way? What could she
mean? To look at her, there was nothing remotely
like an Indian about her. Why claim a thing like
that? I myself had Indian blood in me. My grandmother is a Carib Indian. That makes me one-
quarter Carib Indian. But I don't go around saying
that I have some Indian blood in me. The Carib
Indians were good sailors, but I don't like to be on
the sea; I only like to look at it. To me my grandmother is my grandmother, not an Indian. My
grandmother is alive; the Indians she came from are
all dead. If someone could get away with it, I am
sure they would put my grandmother in a museum,
as an example of something now extinct in nature,
one of a handful still alive. In fact, one of the mu-
seums to which Mariah had taken me devoted a
whole section to people, all dead, who were more
or less related to my grandmother.

Mariah says, "I have Indian blood in me," and
underneath everything I could swear she says it as
if she were announcing her possession of a trophy.

How do you get to be the sort of victor who can claim to be the vanquished also?

I now heard Mariah say, "Well," and she let out a long breath, full of sadness, resignation, even dread. I looked at her; her face was miserable, tormented, ill-looking. She looked at me in a pleading way, as if asking for relief, and I looked back, my face and my eyes hard; no matter what, I would not give it.

I said, "All along I have been wondering how you got to be the way you are. Just how it was that you got to be the way you are."

Even now she couldn't let go, and she reached out, her arms open wide, to give me one of her great hugs. But I stepped out of its path quickly, and she was left holding nothing. I said it again. I said, "How do you get to be that way?" The anguish on her face almost broke my heart, but I would not bend. It was hollow, my triumph, I could feel that, but I held on to it just the same.

THE TONGUE

AT FOURTEEN I had discovered that a tongue had no real taste. I was sucking the tongue of a boy named Tanner, and I was sucking his tongue because I had liked the way his fingers looked on the keys of the piano as he played it, and I had liked the way he looked from the back as he walked across the pasture, and also, when I was close to him, I liked the way behind his ears smelled. Those three things had led to my standing in his sister's room (she was my best friend), my back pressed against the closed door, sucking his tongue. Someone should have told me that there were other things to seek out in a tongue than the flavor of it, for then I would not have been standing there sucking on poor Tanner's tongue as if it were an old Frozen Joy with all its flavor run out and nothing left but the ice. As I was sucking away, I was thinking, Taste is not the thing to seek out in a tongue; how it makes you feel—that is the thing. I used to like to eat boiled cow's tongue served in a sauce of lemon juice, on- ions, cucumber, and pepper; but cow's tongue has no real taste either. It was the sauce that made the cow's tongue so delicious to eat.

At the time I was thinking of Tanner's tongue, I was sitting at the dining table with Miriam, the youngest of Lewis and Mariah's four children, feed- ing her a bowl of stewed plums and yogurt specially prepared for her by her mother. She did not like this, and so to make her eat I told her that she was not really eating stewed fruit and yogurt but a special food that grew in wildflowers and was very much sought after by fairies. I told her that if she ate enough of it, eventually she would be able to see things that other people could not see. This was just the sort of thing my mother used to say to me when I would not eat my food, and just as I did not believe my mother, Miriam did not believe me; she ate, but it was a long, drawn-out process, just as it was a long, drawn-out process when my mother used to feed me. It was in those times when my mother used to feed me that I first began to notice her, really notice her, as if she were a specimen laid out in front of me. I was not Miriam's mother, and, in fact, whenever I fed her and told her these stories, a sort of bribe to get her to do things my way, I always did it in a low voice, so that Mariah would not overhear. Mariah did not believe in this way of doing things. She thought that with children sincerity and straightforwardness, the truth as unvarnished as possible, was the best way. She thought fairy tales were a bad idea, especially ones involving princesses who were awakened from long sleeps upon being kissed by a prince; apparently stories like that would give the children, all girls, the wrong idea about what to expect in the world when they grew up. Her speech on fairy tales always amused me, because I had in my head a long list of things that contributed to wrong expectations in the world, and somehow fairy tales did not make an appearance on it.

It was the beginning of summer and so we were in the house on the Great Lake, the house where Mariah had spent her summers when she was a child and where now, with her husband and children, she spent her summers as an adult. We had all come here right after the children's holidays began. From where Miriam and I sat at the dining table, we could

see Mariah standing over the kitchen sink. The dining room and kitchen were all part of the same
enormous room, and we were far enough away from
Mariah so that if we talked softly all she could hear
was our muffled voices. She stood in front of the
sink, studying some herbs she had grown in pots on
the windowsill. The sun came in through the window, but only as far as the faucets, so that Mariah
was in the semidark, looking at the plants in the
sun. What Miriam might have seen was her beautiful golden mother pouring love over growing
things, a most familiar sight to her five-year-old eyes;
but what I saw was a hollow old woman, all the
blood drained out of her face, her bony nose bonier
than ever, her mouth collapsed as if all the muscles
had been removed, as if it would never break out in
a smile again. Mariah was forty years old. She kept
saying it—"I am forty years old"—alternating between surprise and foreboding. I did not understand
why she felt that way about her age, old and unloved;
a sadness for her overcame me, and I almost started
to cry—I had grown to love her so.

But then Lewis bounded into the room. Lewis
was a lawyer, and I suppose that's why he was always
reading something carefully. Now he carried in his
hand a large newspaper, the pages parted to the

financial section; either he had just gotten off the telephone after having a chat with his stockbroker or he would soon do so. He made a mock animal sound to Miriam and waved the newspaper at me, and he walked over to Mariah and embraced her from behind and licked the side of her neck with his tongue. She leaned her head backward and rested it on his shoulder (she was a little shorter than he, and that looked so wrong; it looks better when a woman is a little taller than her husband), and she sighed and shuddered in pleasure. The whole thing had an air of untruth about it; they didn't mean to do what they were doing at all. It was a show—not for anyone else's benefit, but a show for each other. And how did I know this? I just could tell—that it was a show and not something to be trusted.

I did not feel that I knew Lewis well at all, and I did not want to. I liked him; he told me jokes, he liked to make me laugh. I think he felt sorry for me, because I was so far away from home and all alone. Whenever he heard me speak of my family with bitterness, he said that I spoke about them in that way because I really missed them. He spoke to his own mother every day, but I could not tell if he really liked her. Sometimes he treated me as if I were another one of his daughters, and he would tell me fantastic stories just to see my face as it formed in belief and then fell apart in disbelief. If I said something he thought interesting, he would ask me all sorts of questions and then later bring me books, books that I did not even know existed. He surpassed the usual standard of handsomeness, and his features in profile looked as if they belonged on a coin or a stamp. What was nice about Lewis was that he did not draw your attention to how handsome he was; he didn't draw attention to anything about him. This was a nice trait in a man, and I made a note of it right away. I was not in love with him, nor did I have a crush on him. My sympathies were with Mariah. It was my mother who had told me that I should never take a man's side over a woman's; by that she meant I should never have feelings of possession for another woman's husband. It was from her own experience that she spoke—the experience of having women who had loved my father, and whose love he had not returned, try to kill her, while they left my father without so much as a singed hair on his head.

After Lewis licked Mariah's neck and she leaned against him and sighed and shuddered at the same time, they both stood there, as if stuck together. It was one of those times when you know the events of a lifetime are passing through a person's mind. It's possible that they were thinking about the same things; it's possible that in thinking about the same things they even came to the same conclusions. But to look at them, they seemed as if they couldn't be more apart if they were on separate planets. The room was not exactly filled with silence; I was still feeding Miriam and had just told her that her bowl of stewed fruit and yogurt was really a "potage," and she seemed to like the word as much as I did when at five years old I first found it on a bottle of Marmite. But when the phone rang we all jumped, for the noise filled up the room and had the quality of an alarm, as if it was a warning to leave a building, quick. It was Mariah's best friend, Dinah, reminding her to come to a picnic in honor of some endangered marshland. It must have been my age, but I could see no reason to be so worked up over vanishing marshland.

For a long time I had understood that a sigh and shudder was an appropriate response to a tongue passing along the side of your neck. After I could find nothing unusual in sucking on Tanner's tongue, I noticed that his hands on my breasts, first rubbing delicately and then very hard, produced an exciting feeling. I do not remember how I knew to do this, but I pressed his head down to my chest, and as he licked and sucked my breasts, I thought, This must never stop. At the time, my breasts were the size of droppers, the small dumplings my mother would put in pumpkin soup, but they felt as if they took up my whole body. I thought I could have this feeling only with Tanner and I had to be careful when I thought of his lips on my breasts, for just that, a thought, would make me forget what I was doing. I would sit at my desk in school, I would lie in my bed at night, I would walk down the street, and all the time I would go over and over, very slowly, the times Tanner's mouth would crawl back and forth across my chest. Then I began to think not just of Tanner's mouth on my breasts but other boys' also. One Saturday afternoon I was in the library behind a tin cupboard, looking at some old periodicals that contained articles I needed to read for a botany class. A boy I knew very vaguely—his mother and mine were in the same churchwomen's fellowship—had been sitting at a table nearby, and suddenly he got up, walked over to me, and pressed his lips against mine, hard, so hard that it caused me to feel pain, as if he wanted to leave an imprint. I had two reactions at once: I liked it, and I didn't like it. But after he pulled his head away I did the same thing to him, only now I placed my tongue inside his mouth. The whole thing was more than he had bargained for, and he had to carry his school-bag in such a way as to hide the mess in the front of his trousers. We met this way for a few Saturday afternoons, but he wore his hair in a pompadour style, imitating a popular singer of the time, a singer I did not at all care for, and I eventually found the smell of the brilliantine he wore to keep his hair in place unpleasant. It ended just as it began, without words. I stopped showing up at the library on Saturday afternoons, and when we passed each other on the street he never stopped to ask me why.

The day we arrived at the lake was a very hot day—unusual, everyone said, for that time of year; but for the first time since I had left home I felt happy. It had been six months now, and I knew that I never wanted to live in that place again, but if for some reason I was forced to live there again, I would never accept the harsh judgments made against me by people whose only power to do so was that they had known me from the moment I was born. I had also grown to love the idea of seasons: winter, spring, summer, and autumn. What wonderful names—and, as far as I could see, appropriate. The heat of summer was different from the heat I was used to. That heat made everything in its path long for the shade; the sun was always overhead, as if you might reach up and touch it. It was a heat that bore down on you, first as a warning, then as a punishment, for sins too numerous to count. But this new heat seemed blessed; it was a pleasant conversation piece; it was a contrast to the six months just past. And the days were so long. I was not used to seeing the sun set after eight o'clock and dusk lasting for over an hour after that. It was as if the earth were a character with many different personalities.

Each day, after breakfast, at around ten o'clock or so, the children—Louisa, May, Jane, and Miriam—and I would set out for the lake. I would make a lunch for us, sandwiches, and we would walk there in our bathing suits and shirts—a long walk through a thickly wooded area. The ground was uneven, sometimes going up, sometimes going down, and always we met a congregation of biting insects. The children were used to it, but I was not, and I would complain from beginning to end, coming and going. We could have driven to the lake, but I could not drive. Mariah had specifically requested a girl who could swim and drive a car; but through the correspondence that served as an interview she had got to like me so much that she thought we could work around it.

I carried Miriam on my back. She hated the walk, and after going a short way she looked so miserable that I would give her a ride on my back. I loved Miriam from the moment I met her. She was the first person I had loved in a very long while, and I did not know why. I loved the way she smelled, and I used to sit her on my lap with my head bent over her and breathe her in. She must have reminded me of myself when I was that age, for I treated her the way I remembered my mother treating me then. When I heard her cry out at night, I didn't mind at all getting up to comfort her, and if she didn't want to be alone I would bring her into bed with me; this always seemed to make her feel better, and she would clasp her little arms around my neck as she went back to sleep. Whenever I was away from them, she was the person I missed and thought of all the time. I couldn't explain it. I loved this little girl. And so I didn't mind carrying her through the woods, all forty pounds of her, for fifteen minutes.

I hated walking through the woods; it was gloomy and damp, for the sun could hardly shine through the tops of the trees. Without wanting to,

LUCY

I would imagine that there was someone or something where there was nothing. I was reminded of home. I was reminded that I came from a place where there was no such thing as a "real" thing, because often what seemed to be one thing turned out to be altogether different. When I was at an age where I could still touch my mother with ease, I used to like to sit in her lap and caress a large scar she had on the right side of her face, at the place where her temple and hairline met. When she was a girl growing up in the country, she had to walk a long distance to school, going through part of a rain forest and crossing two small rivers. One day, on her way home, while going through the rain forest, she saw a monkey sitting in a tree. She did not like the way the monkey stared at her, and so she picked up a stone and threw it at the monkey. The stone missed, because the monkey shifted out of its way. This went on for a few days: she passed the monkey and felt that she did not like the way it stared at her, she threw a stone at it, the monkey shifted and missed being struck. One day when she threw the stone, the monkey caught it and threw it back. When the stone struck my mother, the blood poured out of her as if she were not a human being but a goblet with no bottom to it. Everyone thought that she might not stop bleeding until she died, and then that it was a miracle she survived, though the truth lay in her own mother's skill at dealing with such events.

That was just one of many stories I knew about walking through places where trees live, and none of them had a happy outcome. And so as soon as we started our walk through the woods I would strike up a conversation—either with the children or, if they were not interested, with myself. Eventually I got so used to being afraid to walk through the woods that I did it by myself and began to see that there was something beautiful about it; and I had one more thing to add to my expanding world.

When the children and I got to the lake, we would run into the water to cool ourselves off. We would then explore various parts of the beach, eat our lunch, play in the water; I would read to them. Not long after we started our daily routine of going to the lake, we were sitting in the shade of a bush I did not know the name of, looking at people going by. Louisa and May made up stories about them as they passed; the stories were all about what the passerby's life would be like as a certain sort of dog. They were such imaginative and funny stories that I laughed until my jaws ached. We saw a woman coming toward us; she had long black hair that kept falling into her face, and she kept pushing it back with both her hands. They decided she was a Labrador and started to say things about "Labbie." As the woman got closer, we saw that it was their mother's best friend, Dinah. We all started to laugh at the mistake, and Dinah, seeing us, thought it was the pleasure of seeing her that made us laugh so. She was that sort of person—someone who thought her presence made other people beside themselves with happiness.

I had met Dinah the night after we arrived here on our holiday, and I did not like her. This was because the first thing she said to me when Mariah introduced us was "So you are from the islands?" I don't know why, but the way she said it made a fury rise up in me. I was about to respond to her in this way: "Which islands exactly do you mean? The Hawaiian Islands? The islands that make up Indonesia, or what?" And I was going to say it in a voice that I hoped would make her feel like a piece of nothing, which was the way she had made me feel in the first place. But Mariah, who by then knew me so well, started to clear her throat loudly, as if a frog the size of a moon was caught in it. Later, when Mariah and I were having our before-we-turn-in conversa-

tion, she expressed the hope that I would like Dinah.
She said Dinah was a wonderful person—so giving,
so full of love. She said, "What I like the most
about Dinah is how she embraces life." And this
almost rushed out of me: "Yes, you mean your
life. She embraces your life." But I caught myself,
for if Mariah had asked me what I meant I would
not have been able to explain. I did not like the
kind of women Dinah reminded me of. She was
very beautiful and it mattered a great deal to her.
Among the beliefs I held about the world was that
being beautiful should not matter to a woman, because it was one of those things that would go
away—your beauty would go away, and there
wouldn't be anything you could do to bring it back.
I could see that Dinah was attached to her beauty:
she stroked her hair, from the crown of her head all
the way down, constantly; she would put her hands
to her mouth, not in modesty but as a gesture to
draw attention to her lips, which were perfectly
shaped, the sort of lips used in advertisements for
lipstick. I did not like this kind of woman, but it
only showed what a superior person Mariah was that
she saw in Dinah not a woman who envied her but
a friend full of goodness and love.

Dinah now showered the children with affec-

tion—ruffling hair, pinching cheeks, picking Miriam up out of my lap, and ignoring me. To a person
like Dinah, someone in my position is "the girl"—
as in "the girl who takes care of the children." It
would never have occurred to her that I had sized
her up immediately, that I viewed her as a cliché,
a something not to be, a something to rise above, a
something I was very familiar with: a woman in love
with another woman's life, not in a way that inspires
imitation but in a way that inspires envy. I had to
laugh. She had her own husband, she had her own
children (two boys, two girls), she had her own house
in the city and one on the lake—she had the same
things Mariah had, and still she liked Mariah's things
better. How to account for that.

The times that I loved Mariah it was because
she reminded me of my mother. The times that I
did not love Mariah it was because she reminded
me of my mother. She was standing at the kitchen
table, a table she had found in an old farmhouse in
Finland when she accompanied Lewis on a business
trip to Scandinavia and liked so much that she
bought it and had it shipped back home (when she
told me this, it amazed me to think that someone
could find an old piece of kitchen furniture at one

end of the world and like it so much they would go
to so much trouble to make sure it was always in
their possession), surrounded by enormous blooms
of pink and white flowers. I was supposed to be
upstairs giving the children their baths, but seeing
Mariah look so beautiful, I couldn't tear myself
away. How many times had I seen my mother surrounded by plants of one kind or another, arranging
them into some pattern, training them to grow a
certain way; and they were the only times I can
remember my mother serene, motionless, for she
had the ability to appear to be moving even though
she was standing still. Mariah reminded me more
and more of the parts of my mother that I loved.
Her hands were just like my mother's—large, with
long fingers and square fingernails; their hands
looked like instruments for arranging things beau-
tifully. Sometimes, when they wished to make a
point, they would hold their hands in the air, and
suddenly their hands were vessels made for carrying
something special; at other times their hands made
you think they excelled at playing some musical
instrument, though in fact the two of them were
dunces at anything musical. Mariah, now mistaking
my intense study of her for curiosity about the flowers, held them up in the crystal vase in which they

were arranged and said, "Peonies—aren't they gorgeous?" I agreed that they were and said I did not know a climate like this could produce flowers that bloomed like that, bloomed with such abandon, as if there were no tomorrow. Mariah placed the flowers before me and told me to smell them. I did, and I told her that this smell made you want to lie down naked and cover your body with these petals so you could smell this way forever. When I said this, Mariah opened her eyes wide and drew in her breath in a mock-schoolmistress way, and then she laughed so hard she had to put the vase of flowers down, for she was afraid she would break it. This was the sort of time I wished I could have had with my mother, but, for a reason not clear to me, it was not allowed.

Before we came to the lake, Mariah had worried that I would be lonely, that I would feel isolated, that I would miss my friend Peggy. She did not like Peggy. Peggy smoked cigarettes, used slang, wore very tight jeans, did not comb her hair properly or often, wore shiny fake-snakeskin boots, and generally had such an air of mystery that it made people who did not know her well nervous. I had met Peggy in the park once when I was taking Miriam for a walk. Peggy was with her cousin, also an *au pair*, a girl from Ireland. Peggy hated her cousin and only saw her because of family obligation. They were opposites; the cousin was someone who thought a good outward appearance and proper behavior should carry the day. I had seen the cousin a few times with the children she took care of; immediately recognizing each other as foreigners, we tried to form a friendship. It was not a success. Only after Peggy described her to me did I see why. The funny thing was that Peggy and I were not alike, either, but that is just what we liked about each other; what we didn't have in common were things we approved of anyway. She hated to read even a newspaper. She hated sunlight and wore sunshades all the time, even at night and indoors. She hated children and had nothing but hatred and scorn to heap on her own childhood. She hated silence, and she hated sitting still and looking at nothing in particular. She lived at home with her mother and father, and she said that I could never meet them because they were extremely stupid and hated everyone who did not come from Ireland or someplace near there. She carried in her wallet a photograph of three sisters, singers in a group. I could see that she wanted to look like them: always posing her mouth in a pout, trying to give the same impression of a difficult and hard-to-

please woman. But she wasn't a singer, and she
wasn't difficult or hard to please. She worked for the
government, in the motor-registry department,
stamping approval or disapproval on documents as
they passed her way. She lived far from the city
where I lived with Mariah and Lewis, and where
she worked, so she had to travel by train every day.
When I first saw her, she was standing off to one
side, apart from everybody, her shoulders hitched
up and bent forward, sucking in heavily the smoke
of a Lucky Strike cigarette. I recognized the cigarettes
instantly, for they were the same sort my father
smoked. I had never seen anyone female smoke this
kind of cigarette before. It was something I had always wanted to do, and so I started to smoke them
also; I was not good at inhaling the smoke, though,
and soon gave up the whole idea. When her cousin
introduced us, she had lowered her sunshades down
her nose and looked over them at me. She said,
"Hi," and it sounded strange, as if her voice box
were covered over with cobwebs. She started to tell
me about a long trip she had just taken, and then
in the middle of it she stopped and said, "You're
not from Ireland, are you? You talk funny." And I
laughed and laughed, because in a long time that
was the funniest thing anyone had said to me. People

from Ireland, after all, did not look like me. We exchanged telephone numbers, and after that we spoke to each other at least once a day, sometimes more. We saw each other every weekend and sometimes during the week. We told each other everything, even when we knew that the other didn't quite understand what was really meant.

This new friendship of mine drove Mariah crazy. She couldn't tell me what to do, exactly, because she wasn't my parent, but she gave me lectures about what a bad influence a person like Peggy could be. She said that Peggy was never to come to the house and should never be around the children. But one weekend, a Saturday night, after Peggy and I had been carousing around town, going to movies and visiting record stores and buying marijuana and smoking it by ourselves because all the boys we saw we thought were too dangerous to go home with, she missed the last train of the night and so had to sleep with me in my room. I could have asked her to leave early in the morning, before Mariah could find out she was there, but I didn't. I told Mariah about Peggy's missing her train, and Mariah said, "I guess you like Peggy a lot, and, you know, you really should have a friend." This was a way in which Mariah was superior to my mother, for my mother would never come to see that perhaps my needs were more important than her wishes.

Now I missed Peggy, especially from early evening until I went to bed. We tried to talk every day—she would call from her office, on the government telephone—but it wasn't the same. Mariah, noticing how I felt, thought it would be good for me to meet people—her friends and their children who were my age. She and Lewis gave a party.

One of my pastimes at home, my old home, had been to sit and look through a catalogue from which, each year, my father ordered a new felt hat and a pair of dress shoes. In the catalogue were pictures of clothes on mannequins, but the mannequins had no heads or limbs, only torsos. I used to wonder what face would fit on the torso I was looking at, how such a face would look as it broke out in a smile, how it would look back at me if suddenly we were introduced. Now I knew, for these people, all standing there, holding drinks in their hands, reminded me of the catalogue; their clothes, their features, the manner in which they carried themselves were the example all the world should copy. They had names like Peters, Smith, Jones, and Richards—names that were easy on the tongue, names that made the world spin. They had some-

how all been to the islands—by that, they meant
the place where I was from—and had fun there. I
decided not to like them just on that basis; I wished
once again that I came from a place where no
one wanted to go, a place that was filled with slag
and unexpectedly erupting volcanoes, or where a
visitor was turned into a pebble on setting foot there;
somehow it made me ashamed to come from a place
where the only thing to be said about it was "I
had fun when I was there." Dinah came with her
husband and her brother, and it was her brother
that Mariah had really wanted me to meet. She
had said that he was three years older than I was,
that he had just returned from a year of traveling in
Africa and Asia, and that he was awfully worldly
and smart. She did not say he was handsome, and
when I first saw him I couldn't tell, either; but when
we were introduced, the first thing he said to me
was "Where in the West Indies are you from?"
and that is how I came to like him in an important
way.

His name was Hugh. I liked the sound of his
voice, not because it reminded me of anything in
particular—I just liked it. I liked his eyes—they were
a plain brown. I liked his mouth and imagined it
kissing me everywhere; it was just an ordinary

mouth. I liked his hands and imagined them caressing me everywhere; they were not unusual in any way. His hair lay on his head unevenly, like pieces of mercerized cotton cut at random lengths, and it was the color of a warm brown coat. He was about five inches shorter than I was, and I especially liked that. He smelled like sandalwood. I knew this smell because my father had a shaving cream that he used on Sundays, and it was the same scent. As soon as we met, we spoke only to each other. Nothing we said to each other was meant to leave a lasting impression. Eventually, we were sitting on grass behind a huge hedge of wild roses, away from everybody. For a long time we said nothing, and then Hugh said, "Isn't it the most blissful thing in the world to be away from everything you have ever known—to be so far away that you don't even know yourself anymore and you're not sure you ever want to come back to all the things you're a part of?" I knew so well just what he meant, and it made me sigh and press myself against him as if he were the last thing in the world. He kissed me on my face and ears and neck and in my mouth. If I enjoyed myself beyond anything I had known so far, it must have been because such a long time had passed since I had been touched in that way by anyone; it must have been because I was so far from home. I was not in love.

We were still lying on the grass. We had no clothes on. It had gotten quite dark, but the air was still very hot. The wild roses perfumed the air in a sickly but delicious way. I was feeling that I was made up only of good things when suddenly I remembered that I had forgotten to protect myself, something Mariah had told me over and over that I must remember to do. She had taken me to her own doctor, and every time I left the house on an outing with Peggy, Mariah would remind me to make sure I used the things he had given me. My period was due in two weeks, and the thought that it might not show up made me stiffen suddenly. I felt like running, running for the two weeks; at the end of this time, either my period would show up or I would die from exhaustion. I shivered so hard that Hugh noticed and said, "What's the matter?" and pulled me back down next to him. He buried his face in the hair under my arms; he took first one breast, then the other into his mouth as if he meant to swallow them whole. He meant to make me feel again the thing that had just happened between us, but now I was only reminded of my past, filled with confusion and dread.

L U C Y

When I was around twelve years old or so, I was given three yards of cloth as a present. It was an ugly piece of cloth; it had printed on it a design of brown boxes with the word "Pandora" written across each one and a black-haired beast emerging from the open lid. With my mother's permission, I had it made up in a dress not appropriate to wear to church but appropriate to wear to a fete: no sleeves and a sweetheart neck. One day I was putting on that dress, and while my arms were raised high above my head I saw this amazing thing—a brownish, curly patch of hair growing under each arm. I was shocked at this sign of something I thought would never happen to me, a sign that certain parts of my life could no longer be kept secret from my mother, or people in general; anyone could look at me and know things about me. I got a washrag and rubbed hard under my arms, but the hair just stayed there; it would not go away. I had known that, but I could not prevent myself from trying. I then thought that if I had hair growing in one place, perhaps I had hair growing in other places also, and I put my hands in my underpants and felt. My worst fears were true; I had hair growing there also—a patch of small, short curls, like hair on a baby's head. Sometimes, when I would find myself in a mess that left me very disturbed, I would say to myself, I am going to wake up now, and I would wake. But this was not a dream, this was my real life. I was undergoing a change, and there was nothing I could do to stop it. Not long after, I was about to take my bath in preparation for school. I had been feeling odd while going about my morning chores, and had complained to my mother about an ache in my stomach and a chill. I got undressed for my bath. I removed my underpants. My underpants were stained with a rust color, but I didn't recognize this color as blood. It frightened me all the same, and I immediately cried out for my mother to come and help me. When she saw my predicament, she laughed and laughed. It was a kind laugh, a reassuring laugh. And then she said that finding blood in my underpants might be something one day I would get down on my knees and pray for.

I did not spend the next two weeks worrying about my period. If it did not show up, there was no question in my mind that I would force it to do so. I knew how to do this. Without telling me exactly how I might miss a menstrual cycle, my mother had shown me which herbs to pick and boil, and what time of day to drink the potion they produced, to bring on a reluctant period. She had presented the whole idea to me as a way to strengthen the womb, but underneath we both knew that a weak womb was not the cause of a missed period. She knew that I knew, but we presented to each other a face of innocence and politeness and even went so far as to curtsy to each other at the end. The only thing now was that if I did need those herbs, they did not grow where I was and I would have to write to my mother and ask her for them. That would have been hard to do; just my asking for these particular herbs would let her know exactly what I had been up to, and I had always thought I would rather die than let her see me in such a vulnerable position—unmarried and with child.

For the first time in a long time, I began to look forward. It wasn't that I thought each new day would bring unlimited pleasure and happy surprises; I just had a feeling, a wonderful feeling, inside of me. If someone had asked me, I would have had to say, Yes, life isn't so bad after all. It was Mariah who asked me if the source of all this was Hugh— she had caught me whistling—and when I told her no, I could see that she did not altogether believe me. What made sense to her was that if you liked being with someone in that particular way, then you must be in love with him. But I was not in love with Hugh. I could tell that being in love would complicate my life just now. I was only half a year free of some almost unbreakable bonds, and it was not in my heart to make new ones. I could take in all of this very easily. Just thinking about his hands and his mouth could make me feel as if I were made up of an extravagant piece of silk; yet if I were told that he had left unexpectedly on a trip and would not be back for a long time, I would have to say too bad, for I had not yet grown tired of him, and accept it with no more than a shrug of my shoulders. For already I could see ahead to the fifteenth of September, the day when I would bend my knee a little so that I could kiss Hugh's cheek, step into a car, and then wave and wave as it drove away, until he was out of sight. To latch on to this boy—man, I suppose—who liked the way the tightly curled hair on my head and other parts of my body trapped his fingers was not for someone my age, and certainly not for me.

Mariah and Dinah and other people they knew had become upset by what seemed to them the destruction of the surrounding countryside. Many houses had been built on what they said used to be farmland. Mariah showed me a place that had been

an open meadow, a place where as a girl she went
looking for robin's eggs and picking wildflowers. She
moaned against this vanishing idyll so loudly that
Louisa, who was just at the age where if you are a
girl you turn against your mother, said, "Well, what
used to be here before this house we are living in
was built?" It was a question I had wanted to ask,
but I couldn't bear to see the hurt such a question
would bring to Mariah's face.

Mariah decided to write and illustrate a book
on these vanishing things and give any money made
to an organization devoted to saving them. Like her,
all of the members of this organization were well off
but they made no connection between their comforts
and the decline of the world that lay before them.
I could have told them a thing or two about it. I
could have told them how nice it was to see them
getting a small sip of their own bad medicine. Some
days she would go out from early morning until late
afternoon sketching specimens of all sorts in their
various habitats; she gave me the impression that
everything was on its last legs and any day now would
disappear from the face of the earth. Mariah was the
kindest person I had ever known. Her concern was
not an unexpected part of her; it could be said that
her kindness was the result of her comfortable cir-

cumstances, but many people in her position were not as kind and considerate as she was. And that was the reason I couldn't bring myself to point out to her that if all the things she wanted to save in the world were saved, she might find herself in reduced circumstances; I couldn't bring myself to ask her to examine Lewis's daily conversations with his stockbroker, to see if they bore any relation to the things she saw passing away forever before her eyes. Ordinarily that was just the sort of thing I enjoyed doing, but I had grown to love Mariah so much.

Mariah and Lewis had been having a disagreement over what animal was eating the new shoots of a vegetable Lewis had planted in a small patch of dirt that he had turned over and made good for growing vegetables. Lewis really had nothing to do when he was here; he read papers he had sent from the office, and all sorts of books, but being here in a house that overlooked a lake was not his idea. I never got the feeling from him, as I did from Mariah, that this was the only place in the world to be from the middle of June to the middle of September. And so, I suppose to amuse himself, he had made a little garden, and he grew in it green beans, spinach, lettuce, and some tomato plants that bore fruit the size of grapes. He had done this for years now, and always he had enjoyed all the fruits, so to speak, of his labor. But this time, as each little shoot of something made an appearance, an animal would come at night and eat the shoots. Lewis built a fence around the garden, but the animal got under it and ate everything down to the ground. Lewis was sure it was a family of rabbits that Mariah and the children had grown fond of and encouraged to come up into the house.

We were sitting at the dining table, all of us, just finishing a delicious pie of red berries that Mariah had made, when Lewis mentioned again the destruction of his vegetables. Mariah, trying to turn the conversation away from the rabbits, said that a certain sort of bug will slice off the tops of young shoots, but that of course Lewis should avoid pesticides and find a natural antidote, an enemy of this bug. A minute or so went by, allowing the subject of destroyed vegetables to pass from everybody's mind, and then Mariah told, with actual jubilation in her voice, of a sighting of yet another family of rabbits living near the entrance of the driveway; how astonishing and incredible they were, she said, coming up to a few inches from her and looking her right in the eye as if they meant to say something, to tell her the secrets of their existence. Lewis said, "Jesus Christ! The goddam rabbits!" and he made his hands into two fists, lifted them up in the air, and brought them down on the table with such force that everything on the table—eating utensils, plates, cups in saucers, the empty pie dish—rattled and shook as if in an earthquake, and one glass actually tipped over, rolled off the table, and shattered. We all looked at Lewis; in the long silence that followed, that was all we seemed able to do—just look at Lewis. In the silence, a world of something must have appeared; the children were too young to get to the bottom of it, and I was too unfamiliar with a situation like this. But it made Mariah force both her hands into her mouth as if desperate to keep something from coming out. I thought, In the history of civilization, they mention everything; even the water glass shattered on the floor—something is said about that—but there is not one word on the misery to be found at a dining-room table. We all sat there locked up in that moment, and without a doubt it meant something different to everybody, none of it good. The spell was broken by Miriam, who started to cry; she cried and cried, the way children will when they know something is wrong but not exactly what. I picked her up to comfort her, and kissed her little head, but I might as well have been doing all that to myself, for I felt as if I were about to lose something I had just found. I gathered the children, and we went upstairs to my room and played a game of gin rummy.

One day Mariah persuaded Lewis to go to the marshlands with her. This was the day I received the tenth letter from my mother to which I would make no reply; as with the nine others before it, I would not even break the seal on the envelope. I believe I heard them drive away; I believe I heard the sound of the car's wheels on the dirt road; I believe so, but I could not really say for sure; it's possible that I just took those things for granted. Later, I wondered if just the way the car door had sounded as it slammed shut, or the way the car's wheels sounded as they ran over the dirt road, should have told me to expect something. The children and I were getting ready to go to the lake when we heard a scream, and we ran to a window that looked out in the direction from which the scream came. We saw Mariah running back toward the house, crying, her hands moving about in the air as if she were conducting a choir. She ran into the house, and just as we were about to go downstairs to see what was the matter, Lewis came into view. He was walking slowly, and in his hands he carried the limp body of a small animal, a rabbit. He had a funny look on his face; he looked like a boy in a picture, a boy who had placed a live mouse under his mother's saucer and, on getting the desired result, pretended not to know what all the commotion was about. Lewis walked along in this way, and then something made him look up, and he saw our five faces framed behind the large glass-paned window. He stopped for a moment; whatever he saw in his children's faces I do not know, but I suddenly felt sorry for him. He looked lost, unhappy, as if he might remember this as one of the most unhappy days in his entire life.

They buried the rabbit in a ceremony I could not bring myself to attend. The ceremony was another one of those untruths that I had only just begun to see as universal to life with mother, father, and some children. I had thought the untruths in family life belonged exclusively to me and my family, with my mother's unopened letters representing evidence of the most important kind. Mariah and Lewis told the children that the car had run over the rabbit by accident, and they said it in such a way that I could only think they wanted the children to believe the car was driving itself. But when the children were out of the room Mariah would accuse Lewis of running over the rabbit on purpose, and Lewis would say that it really had been an accident, that the very path he took to avoid hitting the rabbit was just where the rabbit ran. Then Mariah would say, "But you aren't sorry that you did it?" and he would say, "No, I am not sorry that it happened." It was an important difference, but in a situation like that, how could Mariah be expected to see it?

Everything remains the same and yet nothing is the same. When this revelation was new to me, years ago, I told it to my mother, and when I saw how deeply familiar she was with it I was speechless. One day, Louisa said to me, after reading a letter from one of her school chums, "My mother and father love each other very much." She said it with such force that I looked at her closely, for I thought she would reveal something. And what made her say that—something in the letter, or something in the air? Hours before, I had walked into a room and heard Mariah say to Lewis, "What's wrong with us?" Then their friend Dinah came in; she was on her daily walk and was stopping by to say hello. Before Dinah came in, Mariah and Lewis had been standing there like two beings from different planets looking for evidence of a common history and finding none. It was horrible. As soon as Dinah came, Lewis's mood changed. He was no longer in the same room with Mariah; he was in the same room with Dinah. Lewis and Dinah started to laugh at the same things, and their peals of laughter would fly up into the air wrapped around each other like a toffee twist. Mariah could not see this and tried to join in, but every time she started a sentence about one thing, they started on another, completely different subject. This all happened very quickly, and probably if I had not disliked Dinah so much I would not have noticed it. But I did notice it, and it seemed important, like a small part of a map, isolated and blown up large in the hope that it might yield a clue. Mariah and I left that room together, but I had forgotten to take with me what I had gone there to get in the first place, and so I went back. I saw Lewis standing behind Dinah, his arms around her shoulders, and he was licking her neck over and over again, and how she liked it. This was not a show, this was something real; and I thought of Mariah and all those books she had filled with photographs that began with when she and Lewis first met, in Paris in the shadow of the Eiffel Tower or in London in the shadow of Big Ben or somewhere foolish like that. Mariah then wore her yellow hair long and

unkempt, and did not shave her legs or underarms,
as a symbol of something, and was not a virgin and
had not been for a long time. And there were pictures
of them getting married against their parents' wishes,
behind their parents' backs, and of their children
just born in hospitals, and birthday parties and trips
to canyons and deserts and mountains, and all sorts
of other events. But here was a picture that no one
would ever take—a picture that would not end up
in one of those books, but a significant picture all
the same.

A woman like Dinah was not unfamiliar to me,
nor was a man like Lewis. Where I came from, it
was well known that some women and all men in
general could not be trusted in certain areas. My
father had perhaps thirty children; he did not know
for sure. He would try to make a count but then he
would give up after a while. One woman he had
children with tried to kill me when I was in my
mother's stomach. She had earlier failed to kill my
mother. My father had lived with another woman
for years and was the father of her three children;
she tried to kill my mother and me many times. My
mother saw an obeah woman every Friday to prevent
these attempts from being successful. When my
mother married my father, he was an old man and

she a young woman. This suited them both. She had someone who would leave her alone yet not cause her to lose face in front of other women; he had someone who would take care of him in his dotage. This was not a situation I hoped to take as an example, but I could see that, in marrying a man, my mother had thought very hard not so much about happiness as about her own peace of mind.

Mariah did not know that Lewis was not in love with her anymore. It was not the sort of thing she could imagine. She could imagine the demise of the fowl of the air, fish in the sea, mankind itself, but not that the only man she had ever loved would no longer love her. She complained about the weather, she complained about all sorts of things that ordinarily she would not have noticed; she criticized my behavior, and then she criticized herself for criticizing me.

I said goodbye to everything one month before we left. I would not miss the lake; it stank anyway, and the fish that lived in it were dying from living in it. I would not miss the long hot days, I would not miss the cool shaded woods, I would not miss the strange birds, I would not miss animals that came out at dusk looking for food—I would not miss any-

thing, for I long ago had decided not to miss anything. I sang songs; they were all about no pot of
gold at the end of the rainbow, no good deed going
unpunished, and unrequited love. I sang the tunes
out loud and kept the words to myself.

I said goodbye to Hugh, though he did not know
it. It was late at night, and we were lying on the
shore of the lake without any clothes on. A large
moon was overhead; it was in a shroud, and so rain
would fall the following day. As I kissed Hugh, my
tongue reaching to caress the roof of his mouth, I
thought of all the other tongues I had held in my
mouth in this way. I was only nineteen, so it was
not a long list yet. There was Tanner, and he was
the first boy with whom I did everything possible
you can do with a boy. The very first time we did
everything we wanted to do, he spread a towel on
the floor of his room for me to lie down on, because
the old springs in his bed made too much noise; it
was a white towel, and when I got up it was stained
with blood. When he saw it, he first froze with fear
and then smiled and said, "Oh," a note too trium-
phant in his voice, and I don't know how but I found
the presence of mind to say, "It's just my period
coming on." I did not care about being a virgin and
had long been looking forward to the day when I

could rid myself of that status, but when I saw how much it mattered to him to be the first boy I had been with, I could not give him such a hold over me. Before that, there was a girl from school I used to kiss, but we were best friends and were only using each other for practice. There was the boy I used to kiss in the library and continued to kiss long after I had ceased to care about him one way or the other, just to see how undone he could become by my kisses. One night my friend Peggy and I, on our rounds in the city, met a boy in a record store and we both thought he was quite interesting to look at, for he reminded us of a singer we liked. We invited him to have a cup of coffee with us, and he accepted, but over the coffee all he talked about was football. Peggy hated sports of any kind, because they reminded her of her father, and I only liked cricket, which was the sport my father played. We were so disappointed that we went back to my room and smoked marijuana and kissed each other until we were exhausted and fell asleep. Her tongue was narrow and pointed and soft. And that was how I said goodbye to Hugh, my arms and legs wrapped tightly around him, my tongue in his mouth, thinking of all the people I had held in this way.

COLD HEART

ALL THE WINDOWS in Lewis and Mariah's apartment had outside them iron bars twisted decoratively into curves and curls, so that if somehow the children should climb up on the windowsill and slip out, they would be unable to fall down from the tenth floor and land on the sidewalk. It was a reasonable thing to do, protect your children's lives, but all the same I was confounded: Couldn't human beings in their position—wealthy, comfortable, beautiful, with the best the world had to offer at their fingertips—be safe and secure and never suffer so much as a broken fingernail?

I was standing at one of those windows in the living room, looking down at the street. It was a cold day in October, and the wind was blowing small bits of rubbish about. As a child in school, I had learned how the earth tilts away from the sun and how that causes the different seasons; even though I was quite young when I learned about this, I had noticed that all the prosperous (and so, certainly, happy) people in the world inhabited the parts of the earth where the year, all three hundred and sixty-five days of it, was divided into four distinct seasons. I was born and grew up in a place that did not seem to be influenced by the tilt of the earth at all; it had only one season—sunny, drought-ridden. And what was the effect on me of growing up in such a place? I did not have a sunny disposition, and, as for actual happiness, I had been experiencing a long drought.

From where I stood at the window, I could see into the apartment across the way. A man and a woman and some children lived there. I had observed them before at various times. I had seen them in bathrobes, in evening clothes, and in ordinary, everyday wear. I had never seen these people do anything interesting—not exchange a kiss, not have what looked like a quarrel. They were always just passing through this room, as if it were a way station. Now it was empty of people. I could see a sofa, two chairs, and a wall of books. How luxurious, I thought, to have an empty room in your house, a room that nobody really needed. And isn't that what everyone in the world should have—more than was needed, one more room than you really need in your house? Not a question I would put to Mariah, for she felt just the opposite. She had too much of everything, and so she longed to have less; less, she was sure, would bring her happiness. To me it was a laugh and a relief to observe the unhappiness that too much can bring; I had been so used to observing the results of too little. This reminded me that lately I had been having the same dream over and over: There was a present for me wrapped up in one of my mother's beautiful madras head-kerchiefs. I did not know what the present itself was, but it was something that would make me exceedingly happy; the only trouble was that it lay at the bottom of a deep, murky pool, and no matter how much water I bailed out I always woke up before I got to the bottom.

It was a Sunday, and I was alone in the apartment. Mariah and Lewis had taken their children somewhere in the country to pick apples. The way they looked as they were leaving—if I had not known, I would have said, "What a happy family!" The children were well dressed, their stomachs filled with a delicious breakfast of muffins that Mariah had made from specially purchased ingredients, and ba-

con and eggs from what could only have been specially cared-for pigs and hens. As they waited for the
elevator to come, they were laughing. Lewis was in
the role of the amusing and adorable father today,
and so he had put on a lion's mask and then said
and done things not expected of a lion. The children,
in response, shrieked and laughed and fell down on
top of each other with pleasure. When the elevator
came, it was hard for them to just calmly go into it,
and Mariah gathered up their coats and gloves and
hats and "shoo-shooed" them, mocking the gesture
of a farm wife to a brood of chicks. All of them,
mother and father and four children, looked healthy,
robust—everything about them solid, authentic; but
I was looking at ruins, and I knew it right then. The
actual fall of this Rome I hoped not to be around
to see, but just in case I could not make my own
quick exit I planned to avert my eyes.

I was waiting for a call from Peggy. Since it
was a Sunday, she had gone to church with her
mother and then to visit an old relative who insisted
on living alone. Peggy was going to call to let me
know what time we should meet in the park. It was
our custom on Sunday afternoons to go for a walk
in the park and look around, then pick out the men
we imagined we would like to sleep with. We would

pay careful attention to their bottoms, their legs, their shoulders, and their faces, especially their mouths. If all passed muster, though, Peggy would put a stop to our making an approach. She would look closely at their hands and say that though everything else seemed acceptable, their hands were too small. She had said to me—with such sincerity I almost thought it something taught to her in catechism class—that if a man had small hands, it meant he had a small penis to match. When she first said this to me, it came as a complete surprise: I had never dreamed that such a thing as a penis did not come in a uniform size. When I then asked her what could a small penis mean to me, she raised her eyebrows and said only, "Disappointment." It soon became clear that I was a failure at judging the size of a man's hand, and so it was left up to Peggy; whenever we went to the park we came home alone, just the two of us.

I did not like Sundays, and this one was not an exception. I could not believe this feeling about Sundays had followed me halfway across the world. I could not explain it, this feeling. What exactly was Sunday meant to be? Always on that day I felt such despair I would have been happy to turn into something as useful as a dishrag. When I was at home, in my parents' house, I used to make a list of all the things that I was quite sure would not follow me if only I could cross the vast ocean that lay before me; I used to think that just a change in venue would banish forever from my life the things I most despised. But that was not to be so. As each day unfolded before me, I could see the sameness in everything; I could see the present take a shape— the shape of my past.

My past was my mother; I could hear her voice, and she spoke to me not in English or the French patois that she sometimes spoke, or in any language that needed help from the tongue; she spoke to me in language anyone female could understand. And I was undeniably that—female. Oh, it was a laugh, for I had spent so much time saying I did not want to be like my mother that I missed the whole story: I was not like my mother—I was my mother. And I could see now why, to the few feeble attempts I made to draw a line between us, her reply always was "You can run away, but you cannot escape the fact that I am your mother, my blood runs in you, I carried you for nine months inside me." How else was I to take such a statement but as a sentence for life in a prison whose bars were stronger than any iron imaginable? I had, at that very moment, a collection of letters from her in my room, nineteen in all, one for every year of my life, unopened. I thought of opening the letters, not to read them but to burn them at the four corners and send them back to her unread. It was an act, I had read somewhere, of one lover rejecting another, but I could not trust myself to go too near them. I knew that if I read only one, I would die from longing for her.

Peggy did not call me from a telephone; she came to the apartment directly. She couldn't wait to get away from her family, she said; they were a bunch of absolutely nothing. How I envied the contempt in her voice, for I could see that her family held no magic over her. We went to the park. As usual, no men with large hands could be found. We went our separate ways, but made plans to speak to each other on the telephone the next day. I went home to my room in Lewis and Mariah's apartment and sat on my bed. I thought of the summer I had just spent. I had come to see the sameness in things that appeared to be different. I had experienced moments of great happiness and a desire to imagine my own future, and at the same time I had had a great disillusionment. But was this not what life should be—some ups and downs instead of a constant dangerous undertow, capable of pulling you under for good?

Right after we had returned from the summer at the lake, I decided I would not attend school at night anymore or study to become a nurse. Whatever my future held, nursing would not be a part of it. I had to wonder what made anyone think a nurse could be made of me. I was not good at taking orders from anyone, not good at waiting on other people. Why did someone not think that I would make a good doctor or a good magistrate or a good someone who runs things? As a child I had always been told what a good mind I had, and though I never believed it myself, it allowed me to cut quite a figure of authority among my peers. A nurse, as far as I could see, was a badly paid person, a person who was forced to be in awe of someone above her (a doctor), a person with cold and rough hands, a person who lived alone and ate badly boiled food because she could not afford a cook, a person who, in the process of easing suffering, caused more suffering (the badly administered injection). I knew such a person. She was a friend of my mother's and had delivered me when I was born. She was a woman my mother respected to her face but had many bad things to say about behind her back. They were: she would never find a man; no man would have her; she carried herself like a strongbox, and from the look on her face a man couldn't find a reason to break in; she had lived alone for so long it was too late to start with a man now. But among the last things my mother had said to me, just before I left, was "Oh, I can just see you in your nurse's uniform. I shall be very proud of you." And I could only guess which nurse's uniform she meant—the uniform made of cloth or the one made of circumstances.

As I sat on that bed, the despair of a Sunday in full bloom, I thought: I am alone in the world, and I shall always be this way—all alone in the world.

I had begun to suffer from violent headaches, exactly like the ones that used to afflict my mother. They would come on suddenly, as if I had been struck by a bolt of lightning, last for a while, and then disappear. They frightened me because I did not know when one would come on, and they frightened me because they reminded me of my mother. One day, in the midst of an argument I was having with her in which I was trying to assert my will and meeting defeat again, I had turned to her and said, "I wish you were dead." I said it with such force that had I said it to anyone else but her, I am sure my wish would have come true. But of course I would not have said such a thing to anyone else, for no one else meant so much to me. Her desire not to please me was greater than my desire to erase her, but it so took her by surprise—my wish for such a thing—that she got a headache, a bad one, and it caused her to take to her bed. This lasted for days, and at night I would hear sounds in our house that made me sure my mother had died and the undertaker had come to take her body away. Each morning when I saw her face again, I trembled inside with joy. And so now when I suffered from these same headaches that no medicine would send away, I would see her face before me, a face that was godlike, for it seemed to know its own origins, to know all the things of which it was made.

My friendship with Peggy was reaching a predictable stalemate; the small differences between us were beginning to loom, sometimes becoming the only thing that mattered—like a grain of sand in the eye. She did not like to read books of any kind. She did not like to go to the museum. Going to the museum had become a passion with me. I did not grow up in a place where there was such a thing, but as soon as I discovered it, that was the only place I liked going out to visit. It was Mariah who had taken me there; she had wanted me to see some paintings by a man, a French man, who had gone halfway across the world to live and had painted pictures of the people he found living there. He had been a banker living a comfortable life with his wife and children, but that did not make him happy; eventually he left them and went to the opposite part of the world, where he was happier. I don't know if Mariah meant me to, but immediately I identified with the yearnings of this man; I understood finding the place you are born in an unbearable prison and wanting something completely different from what you are familiar with, knowing it represents a haven. I wondered about the details of his despair, for I felt it would comfort me to know. Of course his life could be found in the pages of a book; I had just begun to notice that the lives of men always are. He was shown to be a man rebelling against an established order he had found corrupt; and even though he was doomed to defeat—he died an early death —he had the perfume of the hero about him. I was not a man; I was a young woman from the fringes of the world, and when I left my home I had wrapped around my shoulders the mantle of a servant.

L U C Y

I was having a thought not unlike this when, unexpectedly, Mariah came up to me. The look on my face must have shocked her, for she said, "You are a very angry person, aren't you?" and her voice was filled with alarm and pity. Perhaps I should have said something reassuring; perhaps I should have denied it. But I did not. I said, "Of course I am. What do you expect?"

Peggy took me to a party in a neighborhood that I had never visited before. There were fewer streetlights there, the buildings were uncared for, there was rubbish all about, and there were almost no people walking around. None of this frightened me; on the contrary, I found it quite thrilling. We went into a building and climbed up some cement stairs, and then we were in a large room lighted by candles and filled with plants that I knew grew in a rain forest, for I had seen them growing there. The room smelled of myrrh and marijuana. It was a party given by someone she knew from her office, a man from whom she often got the marijuana we smoked. Whatever he did in her office was not what he planned to do for his whole life. He was a painter, and some of his paintings were hanging on the walls. They were paintings of people, some of them women without their clothes on, some of them just faces. None of the paintings was straightforward; instead, the people all looked like their reflections in a pool whose surface had just been disturbed. The colors were strange—not the colors any real person would be, but as if all the deep shades from a paintbox had been carefully mixed together in a way that still left them distinct. Peggy had told me about him. She had told me that he was a pervert. I did not know exactly what she meant by that, and she never told me what he had said or done to make her think so. He might have tried to kiss her; she hated men to kiss her unless their mouths tasted of cigarettes. When we were introduced, he took my hand and kissed me on the cheek. It was the way he greeted women.

His name was Paul. I said, "How are you?" in a small, proper voice, the voice of the girl my mother had hoped I would be: clean, virginal, beyond reproach. But I felt the opposite of that, for when he held my hand and kissed me on the cheek, I felt instantly deliciously strange; I wanted to be naked in a bed with him. And I wanted to see what he really looked like, not his reflection in a pool whose surface had just been disturbed.

It was a party of ten people, including Peggy

and myself. Peggy knew the others in one way or another. I had never met any of them before. This was a part of her life I did not know, and I could see why. They were very chatty people, chatty in a way she did not like: they were talking about the world, they were talking about themselves, and they seemed to take for granted that everything they said mattered. They were artists. I had heard of people in this position. I had never seen an example in the place where I came from. I noticed that mostly they were men. It seemed to be a position that allowed for irresponsibility, so perhaps it was much better suited to men—like the man whose paintings hung in the museum that I liked to visit. Yes, I had heard of these people: they died insane, they died paupers, no one much liked them except other people like themselves. And I thought of all the people in the world I had known who went insane and died, and who drank too much rum and then died, and who were paupers and died, and I wondered if there were any artists among them. Who would have known? And I thought, I am not an artist, but I shall always like to be with the people who stand apart. I had just begun to notice that people who knew the correct way to do things such as hold a teacup, put food on a fork and bring it to their mouth without making a mess on the front of their dress—they were the people responsible for the most misery, the people least likely to end up insane or paupers.

I had smoked quite a bit of marijuana and was feeling quite happy and otherworldly. I was staring at some plants that were growing in pots on a windowsill, plants I knew by the names of cassy and dagger. The cassy I used to eat with fungy and salt fish; it was said to be a vegetable good for cleaning out a person's insides. The dagger we used to pound with a stone until it became stringlike and then plait so that it resembled a long braid of hair; at Christmastime it became part of a clown's costume and would be lashed in the air to make a sound frightening to children. These two plants grew so plentifully where I came from that sometimes they were regarded as a nuisance, weeds, and were dug up and thrown in the rubbish. And now here they were, treasured, sitting in a prominent place in a beautiful room, a special blue light trained on them. And here I was also, a sort of weed in a way, and across the room Paul's eyes, a sparkling blue light, were trained on me; his eyes reminded me of a marble I used to have, my lucky marble, the one that, when I played a game with it, always won.

This is usually the moment when people say

they fall in love, but I did not fall in love. Being in such a state was not something I longed for. It was true that I had seen so little of the world that I hardly knew what I really thought of anything. In any case, as I looked at this man whose eyes reminded me of my winning marble, the question of being in love was not one I wanted to settle then; what I wanted was to be alone in a room with him and naked. He came over and sat next to me; he asked me where I was from; he touched my hair, and I could tell that the texture of it was new to him. I laughed a laugh that I could not believe came out of me; it was a gurgly laugh, a laugh shot full of pleasure and insincerity; it was the laugh of a woman on whom not long ago I would have heaped scorn. It was understood that when everyone left, I would not leave with them.

At that moment I looked up and saw Peggy staring at me with her own blue eyes; they were sparkling also, but with anger. She gestured to me to follow her into the bathroom, and when we got there she said to me, "I told you he's a creep, I told you he's a pervert." When I said, "But I like him," an enormous silence fell between us, the kind of silence that is dangerous between friends, for in it they weigh their past together, and they try to see a future together; they hate their present. It is never happy. Peggy lit a cigarette. Some of her hair had fallen forward into her face; she pushed it back, but it fell forward again. She placed her teeth together and sent a mouthful of smoke toward me. This had never happened before. We had never quarreled. I had never chosen the company of a man over hers. I had never chosen anyone over her. She said, "Can't you see from his hands he's bound to have a small prick?" I wanted to say, "Well, it should fit very nicely in my mouth, then," but I could not bear for that to be the last thing we said to each other, and surely it would have been. I immediately imagined our separately going over the life of our friendship, and all the affection and all the wonderful moments in it coming to a sharp end. I made no reply.

We came out of the bathroom feeling, I suppose, relief that we had avoided a permanent collapse between us, but also knowing that sometime, sooner or later, we would only exist for each other with a faint "Oh, yes . . ." The room was full of laughter; all attention was directed at Paul, whose hands were plunged into a fish tank in an effort to retrieve an earring of rhinestones in the shape of a starfish. It looked strangely at home there, for all the things in the tank—the coral, the vegetation, the sand, even the fish—had looked unreal in the first place. Paul's hands, as they moved about the tank, looked strange also; the flesh looked like bone, and as if it had been placed in a solution that had leached all the life away. And I remembered this:

I used to know a girl named Myrna, whose mother was so cruel that it was as if she were not a mother at all but a wicked stepmother. Perhaps in response to this situation, everything about Myrna refused to attain a normal size: her body, her eyes, her nose, her mouth—even her hair would grow no longer than the length of a fingernail, and she was often described as that "picky-haired girl." Though she lived in the house across from me, we were not friends, but our families shared the same fishermen, Mr. Thomas and Mr. Mathew, and she and I would often stand together under a tree, shading ourselves from the hot sun, waiting for them to return from sea with that day's catch. One day, Mr. Mathew came back in their boat alone; there was no Mr. Thomas, and there were no fish. A squall had sprung up out at sea, and in the midst of it Mr. Thomas had been swept overboard as he was trying to retrieve some fish pots. As Mr. Mathew told the story, he seemed unable to believe what he was saying himself, as if he expected someone to tell him that it had all been a mistake, he had imagined the whole thing. He was so pitiful my heart broke just looking at him. He had been orphaned as a child; his mother and father had died when they were trapped in a sugarcane field that was on fire, and now he was orphaned again, for he and Mr. Thomas had been like parents to each other, as would be expected of two people who depended on each other as much as they did. He then started to cry, and it was such a sorrowful sound. I did not know a man could sound like that. I wanted to say something to him, something that would be comforting and at the same time take his mind away from his sorrow, if only for a moment, but all I could say was "Poor Mr. Thomas, poor Mr. Thomas, and, you know, he would have enjoyed growing old with you so much—just the two of you sitting here mending your nets." As I was saying this, I knew it would have the opposite effect of what I wanted it to have, but I couldn't help myself. I turned away, taking Myrna's arm, and we started to walk home.

We walked along for a while, and then I realized that she was crying quite hard, and that made me feel how wrong I always am about my judgments of other people, because if I had been asked I would have said that Myrna was not capable of feeling great sorrow about Mr. Thomas's death or about too much else, for that matter. And so I put my arm around her shoulders and gave her a squeeze, at the same time saying a lot of nonsense I didn't believe, nonsense about Mr. Thomas going to a better place, nonsense about there being a great and wise purpose behind such a thing as Mr. Thomas's being swept overboard. Her response to this was to push me away with a great big shove, her eyes boiling with anger and contempt. And she told me some things. She told me that she had not been crying for Mr. Thomas at all—she had been crying for herself. She said that she used to meet Thomas (she did not call him "Mr." now) under a breadfruit tree that was near her latrine and near the entrance to the alley that was at the back of her house, and she would stand in the dark, fully clothed but without her panties, and he would put his middle finger up inside her. It never lasted very long, for her mother would become suspicious if she was missing from her house for too long a time. She and Mr. Thomas never spoke about it; often she would go to this place and he would not show up; he never explained. After he had removed his finger from inside her, he would give her sometimes a shilling, sometimes just sixpence; he never told her why it was sometimes more, sometimes less.

She kept the money in an old Ovaltine tin, hidden under the stones in the middle of her mother's stone heap. She said that she had not decided exactly what she was going to do with the money yet, but whatever it would be, she did not yet have enough. She said it was for this she cried: whatever she would eventually do with the money, she did not have enough of it yet.

I, of course, had many feelings about this amazing story—all the predictable ones—but then one feeling came to dominate the others: I was almost overcome with jealousy. Why had such an extraordinary thing happened to her and not to me? Why had Mr. Thomas chosen Myrna as the girl he would meet in secret and place his middle finger up inside her and not me? Myrna spoke of this in a flat, uninterested way, as if all they had done was share a cup of fresh rainwater together. This would have become the experience of my life, the one all others would have to live up to. What a waste! It meant nothing to Myrna; she spoke only of the money, and even so she did not have a plan for what she would do with that. For me, the money would have been beside the point. I am sure I would have given it away; I am sure, in fact, that I would have found a way to steal a shilling or two and give it to Mr.

Thomas to have been in Myrna's shoes. Oh, the injustice of everything. What words did Mr. Thomas use to make this arrangement with her, and why, again, had I not been worthy of hearing them?

I remembered that he had a wide mouth, large lips, and a big wide pink tongue, which could be seen clearly when he laughed—a loud laugh. He had the sort of bloodshot eyes that betrayed a lot of rum-drinking. He smoked so many cigarettes that sometimes when he came to deliver the fish to us, he smelled more of tobacco than he did of the sea. He called me Little Miss. Once, my mother had sent me to his house—the house he and Mr. Mathew shared—with the payment for a week's worth of fish, and when he came to the door and saw that it was me he said, "Oh, my!" and he went back inside, because he wasn't wearing a shirt, just his underpants, which were oversized and made of the same blue chambray as my father's. When he came back, he was wearing an old madras shirt, patched here and there, and he held the cigarette he was smoking behind his back, because since he wasn't my father or a close relative, smoking a cigarette in front of me would show disrespect. He thanked me for the payment, and as I was turning to leave he said, "And how is life treating you, Little Miss? How is school?" And I had replied, "As well as can be expected, sir, as well as can be expected." With that answer, I knew I was being a direct imitation of my mother, and he knew it, too, for he just burst out laughing, and I got a good look at his big tongue and gums and teeth. I felt so embarrassed that I had caused him to laugh so heartily and with such abandon when we were alone that I stumbled away without saying goodbye, and he called after me, "God bless you, Little Miss." It was a way of letting me know that no offense had occurred on either side. That was the Mr. Thomas I knew, a nice man who went to sea and always brought me back the fish I liked, which my mother would then cook in a sauce of lime juice, butter, onions, and green pepper. And, in turn, I suppose he would have said, if he could, that the Little Miss he knew was a teenage girl so beyond reproach in every way that if you asked her a question she would reply in her mother's forty-year-old voice—hardly a prospect for a secret rendezvous.

After Myrna had finished telling me her story, we walked home in silence. There were so many things to say, so many questions to ask, but I didn't know where to start. I was afraid that if I asked one thing I would reveal my feelings and show how fa-

miliar I was with what she had just described. I could
not ask, for instance, "Did it feel great?" which was
really one of the things I most wanted to know. I
might betray that right then I was screaming inside,
*"This should have happened to me! This should have
been me!"* I could have retreated into falseness and
said all the appropriate disapproving things, but I
saw she was beyond condemnation. Our houses were
soon in view, and so I said, mock sympathy on my
face and in my voice, "Did it hurt?" The look she
gave—I was the one who felt like dirt.

That night, as I lay on my bed, of course unable
to sleep, I thought of the events of the day, dwelling
not so much on Mr. Thomas's falling overboard as
on Myrna and Mr. Thomas's meeting in the alley
near the latrine, under the shade of the breadfruit
tree. I imagined her at the end of a long day, after
cooking her family's food, washing their clothes,
getting water from the pipes that were far away from
her house, and in other ways waiting on them hand
and foot, and then finally, after eating her supper,
perhaps pretending to make a visit to the latrine,
waiting in the dark for Mr. Thomas. She had made
no mention of kiss on the hair, fierce tongue in her
ear or mouth, kisses on the neck, hands caressing
breasts. Just his hands between her legs, with one

finger going up inside her. And there I had to stop.
What did Mr. Thomas's hands look like? I did not
know. At the time, I thought it would haunt me
until the day I died. I had never noticed his hands.
I remembered many things about him: his mouth,
his teeth, his gums, even his feet. His feet were big
and broad, with cracks around the heels. I had never
seen a pair of shoes on them. I had once seen him
walking in mud. The mud was soft, and it came
between his toes, four little pats decorating the
ground. But his hands—what did they look like? I
did not know, and I never would know. And so it
was that hands I would come to know very well—
Paul's hands, moving about in the fish tank—reminded me of some other hands lost forever in a
warm sea.

Because Peggy and I were now not getting
along, we naturally started to talk about finding an
apartment in which we would live together. It was
an old story: two people are in love, and then just
at the moment they fall out of love they decide to
marry. Our thoughts went this way: would it not be
nice if Peggy no longer had to take a train each day
back to the house in which she lived with her parents, two people whose views about everything she

found abominable; would it not be nice if I no longer had to live in Mariah and Lewis's apartment and take care of their children, if I could have a life of my own and come and go at my own convenience and when it pleased me? There was nothing wrong with my life as I lived it with Mariah and Lewis, but I could hardly imagine spending the rest of it overseeing their children in one situation or another. And the children would not remain children forever. I began to feel like a dog on a leash, a long leash but a leash all the same. Mariah was like a mother to me, a good mother. If she went to a store to buy herself new things, she thought of me and would bring me something also. Sometimes she paid me more money than it had been agreed I would earn. When I told her how much I enjoyed going to the museum, she gave me my own card of membership. Always she expressed concern for my well-being. I realized again and again how lucky I was to have met her and to work for her and not, for instance, some of her friends. But there was no use pretending: I was not the sort of person who counted blessings; I was the sort of person for whom there could never be enough blessings. Besides, there was something else.

When I was around thirteen or so, my mother

had pointed out to me a girl—her goddaughter, in fact—who had just turned nineteen years of age; my mother had said what a wonderful person this girl was, how she had given her parents such cause to be proud of her, and how, generally speaking, she was a good example to all girls who came after her. I had known this girl close up, and I had come to a different conclusion about her. For my mother used to place me in her care from time to time, hoping, I suppose, that some of her good example would rub off on me. If I did anything she considered bad, she would threaten to give me senna tea, a purgative that caused bad stomach gripes; or she would threaten to put me in a barrel and shut the lid tight and forget about me. When I did things that pleased her, she would bathe me and comb my hair and dress me up in her old clothes, and then she would insist that I go to sleep in a clothes basket lined with clean rags. I was much too big for the basket, but she would force me to lie in it all cramped up until she thought an appropriate time had passed. It was hard to see the difference between the punishments for one set of things and the rewards for others. This girl's name was Maude, Maude Quick, and her father was the head of jails—Her Majesty's Prisons—and I used to think of her as my own personal jailer. I had long ago grown to despise her, and so as soon as my mother finished singing this long Psalm of Maude, I burst out, "When I turn nineteen I will be living at home only if I drop dead." This made my mother fall into a silence—a sadness, really—for she didn't know what to do. It was the beginning of my expressing hatred, hostility, anger toward my parents, sometimes with words, sometimes with deeds. And now it was true, but not true enough to suit me: at nineteen, I was not dead, and I was not living in the home I grew up in. I was living in a home, though, and it was not my own.

A strange calm had come over Mariah and Lewis's apartment. They quarreled constantly but never in my presence. I would return to the apartment after running an errand with the children in tow, and I could smell the disagreement in the air. Something serious had been said. Perhaps it was "I no longer love you." Lewis would have said that, and it was true; he no longer loved Mariah. He would have said it in a kind way, because it is so easy to be kind when you are in his position, the winning-hand position. Always when I came in, Mariah's eyes were in one of the various stages of a cry. Mariah was, after all, not my mother, for anyone who made

my mother cry so much—she would have seen to
that person's demise immediately.

One day Mariah and I were in the kitchen,
seated at the table. This is where we always found
ourselves if we had to talk about anything at all. She
had made me a cup of coffee, strong, with lots of
hot, steaming milk, and she had served it to me in
a large cup, the size of a small bowl. She had learned
to make it that way in France, where she had lived
when she was about my age. I began to tell her about
my life with Paul, which was spent almost entirely
in his bed. I told her everything that we did, all the
small details that to someone with more experience
of the world would have gone unnoticed. There was
much to take note of; except for eating, all the time
we spent together was devoted to sex. I told her what
everything felt like, how surprised I was to be thrilled
by the violence of it (for sometimes it was that,
violent), what an adventure this part of my life had
become, and how much I looked forward to it, because I had not known that such pleasure could exist
and, what was more, be available to me.

I had been speaking in this way for a while
when Mariah interrupted and said, "We have such
bad sex." Those words came as a shock to me, for
I had never thought of that. Bad sex. I wondered

what exactly did she mean. From my mother I had gathered that the experience could leave you feeling indifferent, that during it you might make out the grocery list, pick a style of curtains, memorize a subtle but choice insult for people who imagined themselves above you. But I had never imagined the word "bad" could be applied to it, and as soon as she said it I knew what she meant: it was like wanting a sugar apple and getting a spoiled one; and while you're eating the spoiled one, the memory of a good-tasting one will not go away. Mariah then told me of how, during the time she was my age and living away from home for a summer, she had stayed with a family, friends of her parents, and begun an affair with the husband. It was a disaster. She said, "His erection would grow limp whenever he tried to enter me." She had blamed herself, as only Mariah would; she had thought there was something wrong with her or that she was doing something wrong altogether. She later came to understand that he was an old, impotent man and that he found it easier to blame a young girl for his condition than to face the possibility that in this area he was all washed up. The incident had left a mark, and it always took her a while with a new lover to forget herself completely.

(1 1 5)

I didn't say it, but I thought, Of course what you need right now is to forget yourself completely.

One day a letter arrived for me, and written all over the envelope in my mother's beautiful handwriting was the word URGENT. To me the letter might as well have had written all over it the words "Do not open until doomsday," because I added it to all the unopened letters I had received from home. That day I decided to go and buy a camera. Mariah had given me a book of photographs, because in the museum were some photographs I particularly liked. They were photographs of ordinary people in a countryside doing ordinary things, but for a reason that was not at all clear to me the people and the things they were doing looked extraordinary—as if these people and these things had not existed before. When I told her how much it pleased me to go and look at these pictures, she went out and bought me a book of them. Whenever I had a free moment, I would sit in my room and pore over this book. The people in the photographs reminded me of people I had known—in particular a photograph of one boy. He was wearing short pants, walking along in a jaunty way, and he carried in his arms two large bottles. He reminded me of a boy I used to know, a boy named Cuthbert. He was a distant cousin of mine who lived on another island, and so I never saw him enough to get tired of him. His breath always smelled as if it were morning and he had just got out of bed—stale and moldy. I liked that smell so much that whenever I had to talk to him I used to position myself so that the smell of his breath would come my way. From looking at this book of photographs, I decided to buy myself a camera.

And then something happened that I had not counted on at all. At the store where I bought the camera, the man who sold it to me—he and I went off and spent the rest of the day and half of that night in his bed. The moment we knew it would end up that way was when, as he was handing to me a camera that folded up like a jack-in-the-box, I looked across at his face and said, "You remind me of my father," and he said, "In that case you should kiss me." His reply was a joke, but it confirmed my observation. I waited two hours outside the store for him to finish his work, and then we went to his apartment. On the way, we exchanged the usual information: our names, where we were from, things we liked, things we did not like. His name was Roland; he had been born in Panama, but his parents were from Martinique; he liked the sound of rain falling on tree leaves, it made him feel soothed; he did not like snow. It was information to pass the time, information to avoid awkwardness, information of no real importance, and we knew that. We did not exchange telephone numbers.

I left Roland's bed only because I had told Paul that I would see him later that night. Paul was used to this. Peggy could not stand to be with the two of us, and so I would spend the first part of the evening with her and then go to spend the rest of the night with Paul. Always Peggy and I quarreled before we parted, but we knew we would speak to or see each other the next day. The night was cold; there was a wind. Roland lived on the opposite side of town from Paul, so I took a taxi; it was a half hour's ride away, enough time to bury a secret. At the door I planted a kiss on Paul's mouth with an uncontrollable ardor that I actually did feel—a kiss of treachery, for I could still taste the other man in my mouth. The cold wind had left my lips the texture of stale toast, but he ate me up as if I were a freshly baked cake. He was glad to see me and said, "I love you," and I thought, So that's what that sounds like when someone really means it. I kissed him doubly hard, and instantly I knew it was a mistake, for he mistook

my enthusiasm for his love returned. In the morning, he said that Peggy had called me in the early
part of the evening, wanting to know if I was with
him. His voice was without suspicion. I said, "She's
such a nuisance," and flew into an attack on her
character, as if that were the point. He did not know
that what he wanted was an answer to the question,
Where had I been if I had not been with Peggy or
at home?

The children and I had gone for a walk in the
park, and we returned to the apartment with the
usual sounds of torment and pleasure. Lewis and
Mariah were sitting in their living room, and the
children ran in to greet them. I followed, carrying
my camera, which I now took with me everywhere,
and when I saw them, apart yet closely together,
Mariah's eyes red from tears, a crooked smile on her
face as if she were a child trying to put up a brave
front, I knew that the end was here, the ruin was in
front of me. For a reason that will never be known
to me, I said, "Say 'cheese' " and took a picture.
Lewis said, "Jesus Christ," and he left our company
in anger. Mariah held out her arms and hugged all
four of her children together in a big embrace and
said to me, "I'm sorry."

I thought, Why apologize for a swine. And then I wondered when had I come to think of Lewis as a swine: I had always liked him; he had always been kind to me. And then I knew: he made Mariah cry, and I had taken her side; that was something I would always do. And I could see the manner in which Lewis had left her. It was he who was really leaving, but he would never come right out and tell her so. He was the sort of person—a cultivated man, usually—who cannot speak his mind. It wasn't that speaking frankly had been bred out of him; it was just that a man in his position always knew exactly what he wanted, and so everything was done for him. Sometimes he and I would play a game of checkers. I was pretty good at this game, but I could never beat him. His strategy was to attack in an underhanded way; and, no matter what, I would oblige him by blundering into defeat. Afterward he was kind enough to show me where I had gone wrong. "Sorry," he would say, "next time"; but next time was just the same. He was too clever, that man, and too used to getting his way. He would leave her, but he would make her think that it was she who was leaving him. The children were no longer in the room. Her mouth opened. I knew what she would say before she said it. She said, "I am going to ask Lewis to leave." She looked at me with concern on her face; she put out a hand to me, offering me support. But I was fine. I would not have married a man like Lewis.

I was lying in bed one night. The children were already asleep. The house was quiet. I had draped a small square of false silk over my bedside lamp, and it made the room into a mingling of early dusk and the last remains of a faraway sunset. This reminded me of home, and a peculiar feeling came over me, a combination of happy excitement, expectation, and dread. All around me on the walls of my room were photographs I had taken, in black-and-white, of the children with Mariah, of Mariah all by herself, and of some of the things I had acquired since leaving home. I had no photographs of Lewis and no photographs of myself. I was trying to imitate the mood of the photographs in the book Mariah had given me, and though in that regard I failed completely, I was pleased with them all the same. I had a picture of the children eating toasted marshmallows; a picture of them with their bottoms facing the camera—their way of showing me how disgusted they were with requests for more smiles; a picture of Mariah in the middle of an elaborate preparation of chicken and vegetables cooked slowly in red wine; a picture of my dresser top with my dirty panties and lipstick, an unused sanitary napkin, and an open pocketbook scattered about; a picture of a necklace made of strange seeds, which I had bought from a woman on the street; a picture of a vase I had bought at the museum, a reproduction of one found at the site of a lost civilization. Why is a picture of something real eventually more exciting than the thing itself? I did not yet know the answer to that. I was lying there in a state of no state, almost as if under ether, thinking nothing, feeling nothing. It is a bad way to be—your spirit feels the void and will summon something to come in, usually something bad.

There was a knock, and the door opened. It was Mariah. Someone was there to see me. From the way she said it, I could tell it wasn't someone she knew; I could tell it wasn't good news. I followed Mariah into the living room and saw seated there, in a chair that had too much stuffing, a familiar face, the face of Maude Quick, only now she was a woman. She was still a bully—I could see it in her overstuffed frame, matching the chair she sat in. When she saw me, she stood, growing up and out. She said my name, and I felt as if all the earth's gravity had been gathered and made to center only on me; I was reduced to a tiny speck that weighed a world. She said that she had been home for a few weeks and had returned only yesterday. She said, "Here," and she gave me a blue envelope that had stamped on it PAR AVION, and my name and address written in my mother's handwriting. She said, "Your mother asked me to give you this." She said, "Your father died a month ago now." She said, "It happened all of a sudden. His heart just gave out." She said, "You know, his heart always gave him trouble."

I was silent. I remained silent for a long time. I was thinking, Look at how pleased with herself this person is. I was thinking, Everything she has ever done has brought her such satisfaction: eating, especially eating, sleeping, telling me the things she has just told me.

She said, "Your mother is so sad you never answer her letters. Perhaps you never receive them."

Mariah had not left the room; she had been standing a little bit away from where we were standing. She now came and stood beside me and placed one arm around my shoulders, and with the other she held on to my two hands; she drew me close to her. She must have known that I was about to break apart, and what she was doing was holding me together in one piece, like the series of tin bands that hold a box of goods together if it is being sent far overseas. I stood still in silence. My head ached, my eyes ached, my mouth was dry but I could not swallow, my throat ached, inside my ears was the sound of waves wanting to break free but only dashing themselves against a wall of rocks. I could not cry. I could not speak. I was trying to get the muscles in my face to do what I wanted them to do, trying to gain control over myself.

Maude laughed, a small laugh, the laugh of someone who did not even have to make an effort to be correct. She said, "You remind me of Miss Annie, you really remind me of your mother."

I was dying, and she saved my life. I shall always be grateful to her for that. She could not have known that in one careless sentence she said the only thing that could keep me alive. I said, "I am not like my mother. She and I are not alike. She should not have married my father. She should not have had children. She should not have thrown away her intelligence. She should not have paid so little attention to mine. She should have ignored someone like you. I am not like her at all."

It's possible I said all of this in ancient Greek, for Maude only looked at me and smiled. Mariah left the room—to make us some tea, she said. I sat down. I said, this time in English, "You are looking very well, Maude," and she said, "Yes, I always follow the advice my mother gave me. When I was leaving home for the first time, my mother said to me, 'Maude, eat all your meals at the same time every day. Make sure of that.' " At that point I was beyond even silently heaping scorn on such an incredible piece of nonsense.

Of course she urged me to return home immediately. I made no reply to that, I made no reply to anything she said. She left after bestowing on me her benediction of an embrace; apart from everything else, she left behind her the smell of clove, lime, and rose oil, and this scent almost made me die of homesickness. My mother used to bathe me in water in which the leaves and flowers of these plants had been boiled; this bath was to protect me from evil spirits sent to me by some of the women who had loved my father and whom he had not loved in return.

And how did this business of not returning the love all these women showered on him get started? His mother, after asking his father to bring him up, left for England. He last heard from her when he was twelve years old. She had sent him a pair of shoes for Christmas, black with small holes that made a decorative pattern on the front; they were too big for him when he received them, and so he put them away, but when he next tried them on he had outgrown them. He still had them in his safe, where he kept his money and other private things, and every once in a while he would show them to me. He never told me what she looked like, except that she was a beautiful woman. He would also say that she was a kind woman, but even then I thought he was just speaking to a child and so couldn't tell the real story, his real feelings; for how could a woman be called kind when she had left her own child at five years old, and gotten on a boat and sailed away? He never saw her again, and when he told me about her he had no idea if she was dead or alive. When he was seven, his father left him with his grandmother and went off to build the Panama Canal. My father never saw his father again, either. He and his grandmother slept in the same bed. She used to get up a little before he did to prepare his breakfast, the same routine my mother used to follow and must have followed until he died. One morning his grandmother didn't awake before him, and when he finally awoke he realized that she was lying next to him dead. "She must have died in the middle of the night and I never knew," he would say to me. He never said his grandmother was beautiful or kind, but I could see that she had been devoted to him. My mother was devoted to him. She was devoted to her duties: a clean house, delicious food for us, a clean yard, a small garden of herbs and vegetables, the washing and ironing of our clothes. He must have loved my mother, for he married her—the only woman he married. I long ago thought he married her for her youth and strength, the way someone else would marry for money. He was such a clever man.

I had been holding on so hard to the letter Maude had brought that it had become a part of my body, and I no longer noticed it. When I did, I prayed hard to be indifferent to whatever it might say. I opened it. It repeated the things I already knew. My father had died. It was a month or so ago now. Though for a long time he had suffered from a weak heart, still it was unexpected. I must please come home immediately. But there was something new. My father had died leaving my mother a pauper. He had no money. His safe, where he kept the shoes his mother had sent him and other things valuable to him and where he also kept money, had no money in it. When she went to the bank, his account had no money in it. His account at his gentlemen's lodge had no money in it. He had borrowed so much against his insurance policy that perhaps he owed his insurance company money, and my mother was now responsible for that. My mother had to borrow money to bury him, and because she was a member in good standing the church provided the service for free.

I had been putting away some money for the apartment Peggy and I were planning to share; I took it all and sent it to my mother. Mariah, on hearing this, gave me double what I already had sent, and I sent this along, too. I wrote my mother a letter; it was a cold letter. It matched my heart. It amazed even me, but I sent it all the same. In the letter I asked my mother how she could have married a man who would die and leave her in debt even for his own burial. I pointed out the ways she had betrayed herself. I said I believed she had betrayed me also, and that I knew it to be true even if I couldn't find a concrete example right then. I said that she had acted like a saint, but that since I was living in this real world I had really wanted just a mother. I re-minded her that my whole upbringing had been devoted to preventing me from becoming a slut; I then gave a brief description of my personal life, offering each detail as evidence that my upbringing had been a failure and that, in fact, life as a slut was quite enjoyable, thank you very much. I would not come home now, I said. I would not come home ever.

To all this the saint replied that she would always love me, she would always be my mother, my home would never be anywhere but with her. I burned this letter, along with all the others I had tied up in a neat little bundle that had been resting on my dresser, in Lewis and Mariah's fireplace.

One night, very late, Mariah and I were again sitting in the kitchen. She seemed young and light, I seemed old and leaden. We recognized our present state to be a response to our different situations: she, husbandless; I, fatherless. It was as if we had been reading the last sentences of a very long paragraph and after that the page turned blank. Lewis had left her, but she really thought she had asked him to leave. She said they were getting a divorce; she said the children were in a state of confusion and she was worried about their well-being; she said she felt free. I meant to tell her not to bank on this "free" feeling, that it would vanish like a magic trick; but instead I told her of a ride I had taken to the country with Paul that afternoon. Paul had wanted to show me an old mansion in ruins, formerly the home of a man who had made a great deal of money in the part of the world that I was from, in the sugar industry. I did not know this man, but if he hadn't been already dead I would have wished him so. As we drove along, Paul spoke of the great explorers who had crossed the great seas, not only to find riches, he said, but to feel free, and this search for freedom was part of the whole human situation. Until that moment I had no idea that he had such a hobby—freedom. Along the side of the road were dead animals—deer, raccoons, badgers, squirrels— that had been trying to get from one side to the other when fast-moving cars put a stop to them. I pointed out the dead animals to him. I tried to put a light note in my voice as I said, "On their way to freedom, some people find riches, some people find death," but I did not succeed.

When I finished telling Mariah this, she was silent for a while, and then she said, "Why don't you forgive your mother for whatever it is you feel she has done? Why don't you just go home and tell her you forgive her?" Each word, as she said it, stood out as if it were a separate entity, carved in something solid, something bitter and solid. Her words made me remember how it was that I came to hate my mother, and with the memory came a flood of tears that tasted as if they were juice squeezed from an aloe plant. I was not an only child, but it was almost as if I were ashamed of this, because I had never told anyone, not even Mariah. I was an only child until I was nine years old, and then in the space of five years my mother had three male children; each time a new child was born, my mother and father announced to each other with great seriousness that the new child would go to university in England and study to become a doctor or lawyer or someone who would occupy an important and influential position in society. I did not mind my father saying these things about his sons, his own kind, and leaving me out. My father did not know me at all; I did not expect him to imagine a life for me filled with excitement and triumph. But my mother knew me well, as well as she knew herself: I, at the time, even thought of us as identical; and whenever I saw her eyes fill up with tears at the thought of how proud she would be at some deed her sons had accomplished, I felt a sword go through my heart, for there was no accompanying scenario in which she saw me, her only identical offspring, in a remotely similar situation. To myself I then began to call her Mrs. Judas, and I began to plan a separation from her that even then I suspected would never be complete.

As I was telling Mariah all these things, all sorts of little details of my life on the island where I grew up came back to me: the color of six o'clock in the evening sky on the day I went to call the midwife to assist my mother in the birth of my first brother; the white of the chemise that my mother embroidered for the birth of my second brother; the redness of the red ants that attacked my third brother as he lay in bed next to my mother a day after he was born; the navy blue of the sailor suit my first brother wore when my father took him to a cricket match; the absence of red lipstick on my mother's mouth after they were all born; the day the men from the prison in their black-and-white jail clothes came to cut down a plum tree that grew in our yard, because one of my brothers had almost choked to death swallowing whole a plum he picked up from the ground.

I suddenly had to stop speaking; my mouth was empty, my tongue had collapsed into my throat. I thought I would turn to stone just then. Mariah wanted to rescue me. She spoke of women in society, women in history, women in culture, women everywhere. But I couldn't speak, so I couldn't tell her that my mother was my mother and that society and history and culture and other women in general were something else altogether.

Mariah left the room and came back with a large book and opened it to the first chapter. She gave it to me. I read the first sentence. "Woman? Very simple, say the fanciers of simple formulas: she is a womb, an ovary; she is a female—this word is sufficient to define her." I had to stop. Mariah had completely misinterpreted my situation. My life could not really be explained by this thick book that made my hands hurt as I tried to keep it open. My life was at once something more simple and more complicated than that: for ten of my twenty years, half of my life, I had been mourning the end of a love affair, perhaps the only true love in my whole life I would ever know.

LUCY

IT WAS JANUARY AGAIN; the world was thin and pale and cold again; I was making a new beginning again.

I had been a girl of whom certain things were expected, none of them too bad: a career as a nurse, for example; a sense of duty to my parents; obedience to the law and worship of convention. But in one year of being away from home, that girl had gone out of existence.

The person I had become I did not know very well. Oh, on the outside everything was familiar. My hair was the same, though now I wore it cut close to my head, and this made my face seem almost perfectly round, and so for the first time ever I entertained the idea that I might actually be beautiful. I knew that if I ever decided I was beautiful I would not make too big a thing of it. My eyes were the same. My ears were the same. The other important things about me were the same.

But the things I could not see about myself, the things I could not put my hands on—those things had changed, and I did not yet know them well. I understood that I was inventing myself, and that I was doing this more in the way of a painter than in the way of a scientist. I could not count on precision or calculation; I could only count on intuition. I did not have anything exactly in mind, but when the picture was complete I would know. I did not have position, I did not have money at my disposal. I had memory, I had anger, I had despair.

I was born on an island, a very small island, twelve miles long and eight miles wide; yet when I left it at nineteen years of age I had never set foot on three-quarters of it. I had recently met someone who was born on the other side of the world from me but had visited this island on which my family had lived for generations; this person, a woman, had said to me, "What a beautiful place," and she named a village by the sea and then went on to describe a view that was unknown to me. At the time I was so ashamed I could hardly make a reply, for I had come to believe that people in my position in the world should know everything about the place they are from. I know this: it was discovered by Christopher Columbus in 1493; Columbus never set foot there but only named it in passing, after a church in Spain. He could not have known that he would have so many things to name, and I imagined how hard he had to rack his brain after he ran out of names honoring his benefactors, the saints he cherished, events important to him. A task like that would have killed a thoughtful person, but he went on to live a very long life.

I had realized that the origin of my presence on the island—my ancestral history—was the result of a foul deed; but that was not what made me, at fourteen or so, stand up in school choir practice and say that I did not wish to sing "Rule, Britannia! Britannia, rule the waves; Britons never, never shall be slaves," that I was not a Briton and that until not too long ago I would have been a slave. My action did not create a scandal; instead, my choir mistress only wondered if all their efforts to civilize me over the years would come to nothing in the end. At the time, my reasons were quite straightforward: I disliked the descendants of the Britons for being unbeautiful, for not cooking food well, for wearing ugly clothes, for not liking to really dance, and for not liking real music. If only we had been ruled by the French: they were prettier, much happier in appearance, so much more the kind of people I would have enjoyed being around. I once had a pen pal on a neighboring island, a French island, and even though I could see her island from mine, when we sent correspondence to each other it had to go to the ruler country, thousands of miles away, before reaching its destination. The stamps on her letter were always canceled with the French words for liberty, equality, and fraternity; on mine there were no such words, only the image of a stony-face, sour-mouth woman. I understand the situation better now; I understand that, in spite of those words, my pen pal and I were in the same boat; but still I think those words have a better ring to them than the image of a stony-face, sour-mouth woman.

One day I was a child and then I was not. Everyone told me this: You are no longer a child. I had started to menstruate, I grew breasts, tufts of hair appeared under my arms and between my legs. I grew taller all of a sudden, and it was hard to manage so much new height all at once. One day I was living silently in a personal hell, without anyone to tell what I felt, without even knowing that the feelings I had were possible to have; and then

one day I was not living like that at all. I had begun
to see the past like this: there is a line; you can draw
it yourself, or sometimes it gets drawn for you; either
way, there it is, your past, a collection of people you
used to be and things you used to do. Your past is
the person you no longer are, the situations you are
no longer in.

I used to be nineteen; I used to live in the
household of Lewis and Mariah, and I used to be
the girl who took care of their four children; I used
to stand over the children, four girls, at the street
corner, waiting for the stoplight to change color; I
used to sit on a lakeshore with them; I used to sit
in the kitchen, with the inevitable sun streaming
through the window, with Mariah, drinking coffee
she learned to make in France, and trying to explain
to myself, by speaking to Mariah, how I got to feel
the way I even now feel; I used to see Mariah with
happiness an essential part of her daily existence,
and then, when the perfect world she had known
for so long vanished without warning, I saw sadness
replace it; I used to lie naked in moonlight with a
boy named Hugh; I used to not know who Lewis
was, until one day he revealed himself to be just
another man, an ordinary man, when I saw him in

love with his wife's best friend; I used to be that person, and I used to be in those situations. That was how I had spent the year just past.

One day I was living in the large apartment of Lewis and Mariah (without Lewis, of course, for he had gone to live somewhere else all by himself, allowing a decent amount of time to pass before he gave Mariah the surprise of her life: he had fallen out of love with her because he had fallen in love with her best friend, Dinah), and the next day I was not.

My leaving began on the night I heard my father had died. When I had left my parents, I had said to myself that I never wanted to see them again. These were words said in the way of a child; for a child might want someone dead, might even wish to do the deed herself, but would want the dead person to get up and carry on as before, only without the thing that made the child wish for the death in the first place. I had wished never to see my father again, and my wish had become true: I would never see my father again. I wondered how he looked in the coffin; I wondered who had made the coffin and if it was made of pine or mahogany; I wondered if he had been buried in his blue serge suit, the one he always saved for the special occasion that never

seemed to come—perhaps my mother would have
thought his burial was the special occasion. I had
never imagined my father dying. I had never imagined my parents dying. When I told Mariah this,
she said that no one ever thinks their parents will
die, ever, and I had to suppress the annoyance I felt
at her for once again telling me about everybody
when I told her something about myself. Mariah
said that I was feeling guilty. Guilty! I had always
thought that was a judgment passed on you by others,
and so it was new to me that it could be a judgment
you pass on yourself. Guilty! But I did not feel like
a murderer; I felt like Lucifer, doomed to build
wrong upon wrong.

I had not been opening the letters my mother
had been sending to me for months. In them she
tried to give me a blow-by-blow description of how
quickly the quality of her life had deteriorated since
I had left her, but I only knew this afterward—after
I had learned of my father's death, written to her
and sent her money, and then opened the letter she
sent in reply. For if I had seen those letters sooner,
one way or another I would have died. I would have
died if I did nothing; I would have died if I did
something. I then made a last reply to her, though
she did not know she might never hear from me

again. I told her that I would come home soon, and how sorry I was for everything that had happened to her. I did not say that I loved her. I could not say that. I then told her that the family I was living with (Lewis and Mariah) were moving to another part of town; the address I gave her was one I made up off the top of my head. The moment I did that was the moment I knew I would soon make living with Lewis and Mariah the past.

After that, the days went by too slowly and too quickly: I could not wait to put this period of my life behind me, and each moment felt like a ball of lead; at the same time, I wanted to understand everything that was happening to me, and each day felt like a minute. It was gloomy inside the house, and gloomy outside, too. "The holidays are coming," Mariah said. "The holidays are coming." She should have been happy, but she said it as if she were expecting a funeral. The skies were hard and gray; it rained, and the rain felt like small, hard nails; the sun shone sometimes, but weakly, as if it held a grudge. I noticed how hard and cold and shut up tight the ground was. I noticed this because I used to wish it would just open up and take me in, I felt so bad. If I dropped dead from despair as I was crossing the street, I would just have to lie there in the cold. The ground would refuse me. To die in the cold was more than I could bear. I wanted to die in a hot place. The only hot place I knew was my home. I could not go home, and so I could not die yet.

When I told Mariah that I was leaving, she had said, "It's not a year yet. You are supposed to stay for at least a year." Her voice was full of anger, but I ignored it. It's always hard for the person who is left behind. And even as she said it she must have known how hollow it sounded, for it was only a matter of weeks before it would be a year since I had come to live with her. The reality of her situation was now clear to her: she was a woman whose husband had betrayed her. I wanted to say this to her: "Your situation is an everyday thing. Men behave in this way all the time. The ones who do not behave in this way are the exceptions to the rule." But I knew what her response would have been. She would have said, "What a cliché." She would have said, "What do you know about these things?" And she would have been right; it was a cliché, and I had no personal experience of a thing like that. But all the same, where I came from, every woman knew this cliché, and a man like Lewis would not have been a surprise; his behavior would not have cast a pall over any woman's life. It was expected. Everybody knew that men have no morals, that they do not know how to behave, that they do not know how to treat other people. It was why men like laws so much; it was why they had to invent such things— they need a guide. When they are not sure what to do, they consult this guide. If the guide gives them advice they don't like, they change the guide. This was something I knew; why didn't Mariah know it also? And if I were to tell it to her she would only show me a book she had somewhere which contradicted everything I said—a book most likely written by a woman who understood absolutely nothing.

The holidays came, and they did feel like a funeral because so many things had died. For the children's sake, she and Lewis put up a good front. He came and went, doing all the things he would have done if he were still living with them. He bought the fir tree, bought the children the presents they wanted, bought Mariah a coat made up from the skins of a small pesty animal who lived in the ground. She, of course, hated it, but for appearances' sake she kept her opinion to herself. He must have forgotten that she was not the sort of person who would wear the skin of another being if she could help it. Or perhaps in the rush of things he gave his old love his new love's present. Mariah gave me a necklace made up of pretty porcelain beads and small polished balls of wood. She said it was the handiwork of someone in Africa. It was the most beautiful thing anyone had ever given me.

The New Year came, and I was going somewhere new again. I gathered my things together; I had a lot more than when I first came. I had new clothes, all better suited to this new climate I now lived in. I had a camera and prints of the photographs I had taken, prints I had made myself. But mostly I had books—so many books, and they were mine; I would not have to part with them. It had always been a dream of mine to just own a lot of books, to never part with a book once I had read it. So there they were, resting nicely in small boxes— my own books, the books that I had read. Mariah spoke to me harshly all the time now, and she began to make up rules which she insisted that I follow; and I did, for after all, what else could she do? It was a last resort for her—insisting that I be the servant and she the master. She used to insist that we be friends, but that had apparently not worked out very well; now I was leaving. The master business did not become her at all, and it made me sad to see her that way. Still, it made me remember what

my mother had said to me many times: for my whole
life I should make sure the roof over my head was
my own; such a thing was important, especially if
you were a woman.

On the day I actually left, there was no sun;
the sky had shut it out tightly. It was a Saturday.
Lewis had taken the children to eat snails at a French
restaurant. All four of them liked such things—and
just as well, for that went with the life they were
expected to lead eventually. Mariah helped me put
my things in a taxi. It was a cold goodbye on her
part. Her voice and her face were stony. She did not
hug me. I did not take any of this personally; some-
day we would be friends again. I was numb, but it
was from not knowing just what this new life would
hold for me.

The next day I woke up in a new bed, and it
was my own. I had bought it with my money. The
roof over my head was my own—that is, as long as
I could afford to pay the rent for it. The curtains at
my windows had loud, showy flowers printed on
them; I had chosen this pattern over a calico that
the lady in the cloth store had recommended. It did
look vulgar in this climate, but it would have been
just right in the climate I came from. Through the

curtains I could see that the day was just like the one before: gray, the sky shut up tight, the sun locked out. I knew then that even though I would always notice the absence or presence of the sun, even though I would always prefer a sunny day to a day without sun, I would get used to it; I wouldn't make an important decision based on the weather.

It was Peggy who had found the apartment. We were then still best friends. We had nothing in common except that we felt at ease in each other's company. From the moment we met we had recognized in each other the same restlessness, the same dissatisfaction with our surroundings, the same skin-doesn't-fit-ness. That was as far as it went. We had accepted each other's shortcomings and differences; then, just when we began to feel the yoke of each other's companionship, just when we began to feel the beginnings of what might eventually lead to life-long loathing, we decided to move in together. It could have been worse. People marry at times like that; they then have ten children, live under the same roof for years and years, eventually die and arrange to be buried side by side. We only signed our names to a two-year lease.

It was a Sunday. I could hear church bells ringing. I had not been to church in over a year—

not since leaving home. I supposed I still believed in God; after all, what else could I do? But no longer could I ask God what to do, since the answer, I was sure, would not suit me. I could do what suited me now, as long as I could pay for it. "As long as I could pay for it." That phrase soon became the tail that wagged my dog. If I had died then, it should have been my epitaph.

Peggy, who had been living with her parents all along, decided not to do so anymore. She said that she was sick of them. She said it as if her parents were a style of dressing she had outgrown. I had never heard anyone speak of their parents in this way; I never even knew you could make them seem trivial, trinketlike, mere pests. I was not sure whether to admire her or feel sorry for her because she hadn't got parents whose personalities were on a larger scale, parents whose presence you are reminded of with each breath you take. Someone had told Peggy about this vacancy; it had two bedrooms, a sitting room, a kitchen, and a bathroom. I had spent my entire life not knowing the luxury of plumbing, hot and cold tap water, the privacy to be had by closing the door and taking off your clothes and stepping into a bathtub and staying there for as long as it pleased you. I could very well have gone through my entire life without knowledge of such things, and on my list of unhappinesses this would not have made an appearance. But not so anymore. When I saw that the apartment had only one bathroom, I made note of it with disappointment. At Mariah and Lewis's house I had my own bathroom, and my smells were known only to me. Here the windows in the back had bars—not the decorative kind to keep children from falling out, but the crisscross kind to keep people who meant us no good from coming in; the windows in the front allowed the sun, when it shone, to come in plenty. I used to lie in my bed at home, surrounded by all the things they say make for a contented life—a loving family, a safe full of food, harmonious surroundings—and not feel contented. I longed then to live in a place like this: bars on the windows to keep out people who might wish to do me harm, an unfriendly climate, uncertainty at every turn. History is full of great events; when the great events are said and done, there will always be someone, a little person, unhappy, dissatisfied, discontented, not at home in her own skin, ready to stir up a whole new set of great events again. I was not such a person, able to put in motion a set of great events, but I understood the phenomenon all the same.

LUCY

There were many Sundays when I wished I could just lie in bed and not get up for anything, especially not for church. It was a Sunday, I was lying in bed, and I would get up only if I wished to. On the wall in front of me was a photograph I had taken with a camera borrowed from Hugh; it was of a body of water, the lake where I had spent the summer; there was nothing in the picture—there were no boats, no people, no signs of life—except the water, its surface of uniformly shaped ripplets, its depths dark, treacherous, and uninviting. It was the opposite of the water I was surrounded by on the island where I grew up. That water was three shades of blue, calm, inviting, warm; I had taken it for granted, so much so that it became one of the things I cursed.

Mariah had given me a small desk with many drawers. I had placed it near my bed, with a lamp on it. I reached into the top drawer and retrieved a small stack of official documents: my passport, my immigration card, my permission-to-work card, my birth certificate, and a copy of the lease to the apartment. These documents showed everything about me, and yet they showed nothing about me. They showed where I was born. They showed that I was born on the twenty-fifth of May 1949. They showed how tall I was. They showed that my skin and my eyes were the same color, brown, though they did not say if the shades were identical. These documents all said that my name was Lucy—Lucy Josephine Potter. I used to hate all three of those names. I was named Josephine after my mother's uncle Mr. Joseph, because he was rich, from money he had made in sugar in Cuba, and it was thought that he would remember the honor and leave something for me in his will. But when he died it was discovered that he had lost his fortune a while before and did not even have a roof over his head; he had been living in an old tomb in the Anglican churchyard. The Potter must have come from the Englishman who owned my ancestors when they were slaves; no one really knew, and I could hardly blame them for not caring to find out. The Lucy was the only part of my name that I would have cared to hold on to. When I had first begun to think of the significance of my three names, I disliked the name Lucy, because it seemed slight, without substance, not at all the person I thought I would like to be even then. In my own mind, I called myself other names: Emily, Charlotte, Jane. They were the names of the authoresses whose books I loved. I eventually settled on the name Enid, after the authoress Enid Blyton, because that name seemed the most unusual of all the names I thought of. One day when it was firm in my mind that the name Enid was the name I wanted to be known by, I told my mother. I said, "I do not like my name, Lucy. I want to change it to Enid. I like that name better." The moment I said this, she turned a dark color, the color of boiling blood. She turned toward me, and she was no longer my mother—she was a ball of fury, large, like a god. I wondered then, for the millionth time, how it came to be that of all the mothers in the world mine was not an ordinary human being but something from an ancient book. Not long after that I learned, through my usual habit of eavesdropping on conversations between my mother and her friends, that a woman with whom my father had had a child and who had tried to kill my mother and me through obeah was named Enid. I had never heard of that Enid before. When the mystery of my mother's behavior became clear to me, I felt ashamed of the mistake I had made. Even to hurt my mother I would not have wanted the same name as the woman who had tried to kill my mother and me.

Much later, when I no longer cared how I made her feel, I brought up the question of my name again. My mother was stooped over a bowl of fish, cleaning and seasoning them in preparation for our supper. She was pregnant with the last of her children. She did not want to be pregnant and three times had tried to throw away the child, but all her methods had failed and she remained pregnant. An old brown-and-white dog had become attached to her. We didn't know where the dog had come from—only that whenever my mother left our house it was always waiting outside and would follow only her. She did not like animals; where she came from, sometimes when someone wanted to harm someone else they sent the harm in the shape of an animal. When she saw the dog follow her around, she was sure it was something bad, and so she tried everything to get rid of it, but the dog would not go away. She stopped trying to get rid of the dog the day she realized that the dog was pregnant also. It was funny to see them walking down the street together—two female beings, a human and a dog, both of them pregnant. They went everywhere together, and they grew to look alike: thin, shriveled, undernourished (my mother had no appetite), unmaternal. They both became bad-tempered and would snarl at anyone who did anything they found offensive. As my mother was cleaning the fish, the dog was standing nearby, snapping at flies that were bothering her.

LUCY

They made such a picture: the dead fish, the flies, the pregnant woman, the pregnant dog.

It was this sight that was before me when I asked my mother why she had named me Lucy. The first time I asked, she made no reply, pretending that she had not heard me. I asked again, and this time under her breath she said, "I named you after Satan himself. Lucy, short for Lucifer. What a botheration from the moment you were conceived." I not only heard it quite clearly when she said it but I heard the words before they came out of her mouth. And yet I said, "What did you say?" But she wouldn't repeat it; she only said, "Why do you torment me so?" and wouldn't speak to me anymore. In the minute or so it took for all this to transpire, I went from feeling burdened and old and tired to feeling light, new, clean. I was transformed from failure to triumph. It was the moment I knew who I was. When I was quite young and just being taught to read, the books I was taught to read from were the Bible, *Paradise Lost*, and some plays by William Shakespeare. I knew well the Book of Genesis, and from time to time I had been made to memorize parts of *Paradise Lost*. The stories of the fallen were well known to me, but I had not known that my own situation could even distantly be related to

them. Lucy, a girl's name for Lucifer. That my
mother would have found me devil-like did not surprise me, for I often thought of her as god-like, and
are not the children of gods devils? I did not grow
to like the name Lucy—I would have much preferred to be called Lucifer outright—but whenever
I saw my name I always reached out to give it a
strong embrace.

I got out of bed and stood on an old rug Mariah
had given me. I wanted to stretch my arms up and
out, but the room was cold, so I hugged myself. I
walked through the apartment. Peggy was still asleep
in her room; I could hear her snoring through her
closed door. She had once gone to church every
Sunday morning with her parents, and now said she
would never do that again. In the bathroom I looked
at my face in the mirror. I was twenty years old—
not a long time to be alive—and yet there was not
an ounce of innocence on my face. If I did not know
everything yet, I would not be afraid to know *everything* as it came up. That life might be cold and
hard would not surprise me.

I went to stare out the front window. When I
looked down, I could see people, not as many as on
a weekday, bustling about. I could see the roofs of

other buildings far away. I could not see any trees. Everything I could see looked unreal to me; everything I could see made me feel I would never be part of it, never penetrate to the inside, never be taken in. A building across the way had a tower with a clock. I stared at the clock for a long time before I realized that it was broken, and it made me even more conscious of a feeling I had constantly now: my sense of time had changed, and I did not know if the day went by too quickly or too slowly.

Peggy came to look out the window, too. Was she seeing the same things as we looked out on the same view? Probably not. In the less than twenty-four hours we had been together under the same roof, our differences had been piling up. She preferred food that came in a tin, or already prepared, to food she had to cook herself. In general, she preferred having things done for her. She did not even know how to sew on a button. As she stood next to me at the window, she smelled of cigarettes and old food; she had not yet taken a bath or brushed her teeth. She rested her head on my shoulder and said, "Can you believe this? Can you believe we did it?" Her hair smelled of lemons—not real lemons, not lemons as I knew them to smell, not the sort of lemons that grew in my yard at home, but artificial

lemons, made up in a laboratory. Peggy did not know
what a real lemon smelled like. How am I going to
get out of this?—the thought was welling up inside
me, but I quickly placed a big rock on top of it. She
lit a cigarette; I wished she had not done that. She
wanted to make us cups of instant coffee, but I made
us coffee with steaming-hot milk, the way Mariah
had shown me. The afternoon passed. For a very
long moment, I wondered what my mother was
doing just then, and I saw her face; it was the face
she used to have when she loved me without reservation.

Early that evening, Paul came by to see the
apartment for the first time and to take us out to
dinner. He brought us a large bouquet of small yellow roses, and he gave me a photograph he had
taken of me standing over a boiling pot of food. In
the picture I was naked from the waist up; a piece
of cloth, wrapped around me, covered me from the
waist down. That was the moment he got the idea
he possessed me in a certain way, and that was the
moment I grew tired of him. I had been singing a
song out loud. The words were: "Your crazy, crazy
love / Is what I am dreaming of." He thought I was
in a certain state of mind, having to do only with
him. But it was just a song I was singing; I meant

nothing at all. He kissed me now in that possessive way, lingering over my mouth, pressing my whole body into his; and though I was not unmoved, it was not as special as he believed. I knew him better than he realized. He loved ruins; he loved the past but only if it had ended on a sad note, from a lofty beginning to a gradual, rotten decline; he loved things that came from far away and had a mysterious history. I could have told him that I had sized him up, but it was not as if he were going to matter to me for years and years to come. He took us to a restaurant where they served macaroni in many sizes and shapes and with all sorts of sauces, only it wasn't called macaroni but a name foreign to me, and so I felt false saying it that way. We went back to the apartment, and I realized when I crossed the threshold that I did not think of it as home, only as the place where I now lived. Paul stayed in my bed with me. I had never had a man stay with me in my own bed. If I had imagined that such a thing would be a desirable landmark, it meant not much to me now; I only made a note of it.

On that Monday I started a new job. When I told Mariah that I was leaving, I did not know what

I would do. In fact, there was nothing I could really do. I had no experience, except being a student and a nursemaid. But I was not afraid. Somehow I was not afraid. Paul knew a man who took pictures of food and other things with no life any longer in them, and the photographs were sold to magazines. This man said he would pay me a salary for answering his telephone, taking messages, answering correspondence, and running errands. It was a small salary, but I was grateful all the same. Peggy had been preparing me for the world of employee-employer relationships. She had shown me how to behave when applying for a job, how to show the proper amount of respect, submission, eagerness to please, even though in my heart I would not mean any of those things; she said that as soon as I had the job and was safely in it, I could let my real personality come out. I was not opposed to deception, but I would have preferred not to start out that way.

That Monday morning was like many to come, as the rest of the day was like many to come also. Peggy and I silently made our arrangements for time in the bathroom, time in front of the full-length mirror in the passageway, time in the kitchen preparing our breakfasts. At the corner, she hugged me, kissed my cheek, and wished me good luck. Something in that moment, something buried underneath, made tears come to our eyes, but before they could spill out we turned and went our separate ways. I walked along the streets, trying to hold my head up and observe everything, wanting to remember how everything looked and felt, but I knew even then that later on the things that would stick in my mind were not the things my eyes were fixed on. I got to my job, I said good morning to everyone, I sat at my desk. I was now living a life I had always wanted to live. I was living apart from my family in a place where no one knew much about me; almost no one knew even my name, and I was free more or less to come and go as pleased me. The feeling of bliss, the feeling of happiness, the feeling of longing fulfilled that I had thought would come with this situation was nowhere to be found inside me.

The man I worked for was named Timothy Simon. I called him Mr. Simon, not Tim, or even Timothy, as he begged me to do; this made him not call me "honey," or "darling," the two endearments he used when addressing any woman. He was a friend of my friend, he said, and so he and I should be friends also. But I did not know men very well then; the things I did know about them were not so very good. Friendship is a simple thing, and yet complicated; friendship is on the surface, something natural, something taken for granted, and yet underneath one could find worlds. We did not become friends, but he interested me all the same. For he was the first person I had met who had deeply compromised himself. He did not want to be in a studio taking photographs of things with the life gone out of them; he had wanted to roam the world taking photographs of people who had suffered horribly and through no fault of their own. But the market for the work he really wanted to do was limited, he said, and this work that he did paid the bills. After he had said the word "bills" he pressed his lips together into one of those smiles that is not a smile at all but a way of warding off further inquiry.

Each morning I got up and had a breakfast that was becoming flimsier and flimsier until eventually it amounted to just a cup of tea. Peggy and I walked together as far as the corner and then parted, she heading north, I south. At the studio I performed my chores, some of them better than others; my typing skills, for instance, did not exist, but everyone agreed that I answered the phone better than it had ever been answered before. I took up the custom of drinking coffee all the time, though it tasted more like soiled water than the coffee I was used to. I ate lunches of cold moist food, sandwiches, or something that was a combination of gelatin and soured milk; I was sure none of it was good for me, and I liked that.

Mr. Simon allowed me to develop film in his darkroom when he was not using it. I did this in my own time. I had continued to take photographs, but I had no idea why. I even put aside a small amount of the money I earned so that I could take a course at night at a nearby university, but it was not with any ideas about my life in mind—it was only that I enjoyed doing this. Sometimes I would stay late at night, working in the darkroom, trying to get right a print of something I had made a snap of. I mostly liked to take pictures of people walking on the street. They were not pictures of individuals, just scenes of people walking about, hurrying to somewhere. I did not know them, and I did not care to. I would try and try to make a print that made more beautiful the thing I thought I had seen, that would reveal to me some of the things I had not seen, but I did not succeed.

I would walk home alone at night, the air a little thicker, a little warmer than when I had first started on this new phase of my life, for the winter had gone away. At home Peggy was already in her robe, her hair washed and smelling of that false lemon scent. She washed her hair every night and then slept with it wet to get an effect she wanted the next morning. It was after the first time I had come home and met her like this that she had told me she hoped to go to school to study hairdressing and beauty secrets. The way she put it, though, I found very touching, for she made it sound as if she were really going into public service. I knew then that I could never discuss with her my printmaking diffi- culties. Sometimes Paul would be there waiting for me; he waited for me in my bed, because Peggy felt his presence encroached on her privacy. I knew just what she meant. His presence in my bed was often not what I wanted at all, but unless a final goodbye came from him I had had enough of partings just now.

I was alone in the world. It was not a small accomplishment. I thought I would die doing it. I was not happy, but that seemed too much to ask for.

L U C Y

I had seen Mariah. She had asked me to come and have dinner with her. We were friends again; we said how much we missed each other's company. She looked even more thin than usual. She was alone, and she felt lonely. She lived with her four children, but children are not companions. She was going away, she said, far away, to live in a place of uncommon natural beauty. Everyone who lived in this place, she said, was filled with love and trust and greeted each other with the word "Peace." We sat on the floor and ate our food. Around us were some of the remains of her marriage: wine and water goblets made from crystal, china plates decorated with real gold around the edges, real silverware. She was giving all of this away, along with many other things from her married life. She told me to take anything I wanted, but I wanted nothing. I could not imagine living with any of it; everything she had reminded me, as it must have reminded her, too, of the weight of the world. As a present, she gave me a notebook she had bought in Italy a long time before. She found it while going through her old things. The cover was of leather, dyed blood red, and the pages were white and smooth like milk. Around the time I was leaving her for the life I now led, I had said to her that my life stretched out ahead of me like a book of blank pages. As she gave me the book, she reminded me of that; and in the way so typical of her, the way that I had come to love, she spoke of women, journals, and, of course, history. When we said goodbye, I did not know if I would ever see her again.

I was alone at home one night. Peggy was on an outing by herself. Paul was on an outing by himself. I had noticed that this happened more and more; the two of them were busy at something, and I suspected it was with each other. I only hoped they would not get angry and disrupt my life when they realized I did not care. I did all sorts of little things: I washed my underwear, scrubbed the stove, washed the bathroom floor, trimmed my nails, arranged my dresser, made sure I had enough sanitary napkins. When I got into bed, I lay there with the light on for a long time doing nothing. Then I saw the book Mariah had given me. It was on the night table next to my bed. Beside it lay my fountain pen full of beautiful blue ink. I picked up both, and I opened the book. At the top of the page I wrote my full name: Lucy Josephine Potter. At the sight of it, many thoughts rushed through me, but I could write down only this: "I wish I could love someone so much that I would die from it." And then as I looked at this sentence a great wave of shame came over me and I wept and wept so much that the tears fell on the page and caused all the words to become one great big blur.